HEIR OF
THE DOG

Liars and Vampires
Book 6

Robert J. Crane
with Lauren Harper

Heir of the Dog
Liars and Vampires, Book 6

Robert J. Crane
with Lauren Harper
Copyright © 2019 Ostiagard Press
All Rights Reserved.

1st Edition

Chapter 1

I wanted to meet the teacher that invented quizzes. Pop quizzes, chapter quizzes, midterm quizzes. Not to shake their hand or anything. No, I wanted to give them a good smack upside the head for inventing such an acute form of torture for students all over the country.

I mean, what did they accomplish? Did they really teach us anything? Or were they just an insignificant numerical value placed on material that we'd memorized and would definitely forget before the end of the week?

I didn't know. But it was all I could think about. Not the equations and square roots and quadrilateral triangles. I'd made peace long ago with the fact that I was never to be a mathematician...no matter how much my math league teacher had said I could if I tried hard enough.

I huffed and my chin sank into my palm. My eyes glanced at the clock. I was really starting to think that the batteries were dead. It hadn't moved for like a thousand hours.

There weren't even two weeks of school left and the oppressive heat was a constant reminder that summer vacation was just on the horizon. When everyone told me that I wouldn't understand a Florida summer until I experienced it, I had just rolled my eyes. New York could get to a balmy ninety on some days. It was rare, but it wasn't like we wore parkas on the regular.

Turns out, I had literally no understanding about what real heat and humidity was. It was like my skin was melting, coming off in buckets of sweat. I was drinking more water than I had ever consumed in my life and realizing that having a pool in my backyard was the biggest blessing in disguise. Hardly an afternoon went by when I wasn't in that thing.

Xandra was there most days, too, since she didn't have a pool at her house.

At least, I thought with a sigh, that's how it used to be…before our house caught on fire. Now I had to suffer inside, staring longingly outside at the backyard of the rental house we were staying at, wondering who in their right mind didn't install a pool.

Mom kept telling me to just go down to the community pool and I told her I wanted nothing to do with a pool where every child in the development had access, because who knew what might be in that water. I'd rather sit underneath the air conditioning vents and pray the builders would hurry up so we could go back home.

I tapped my pencil on the desk, watching the rest of my classmates struggle against the strain of the heat mingling with the difficult quiz questions in front of them. The air conditioning was having a hard time keeping up this late in the day.

Miss Patterson, our math teacher, was sipping some ice water at her desk. She was combing through the quizzes that the overachievers had already finished.

I licked my dry lips. Just a little bit longer and I'd be able to go home and have some lemonade and ramen.

I blamed Xandra for my newfound ramen addiction.

Everyone looked up when the phone beside the door rang. One of the few places that still had a landline and it was the primary form of communication between the different rooms and the office inside the school. How archaic, especially since the teachers were all texting each other anyways.

Miss Patterson stood up, brushing some of her dark, straight hair from her eyes. I watched as she walked over to the phone, lifted it off the receiver and answered.

A moment of tension passed over me as I watched her face. I half expected her to turn around and look over at me.

Life had been too crazy as of late to rule out the possibility.

When I realized that it wasn't for me, I relaxed. With a heavy sigh, I looked back down at my quiz, which was still only half done. For some reason, I couldn't find the angle to that stupid trapezoid. Then I still had to find the area. I was going to be glued to this desk for the rest of my life.

"All right, I'll let him know," Miss Patterson said.

There was a blip on my radar as I heard the unease in her voice. She hung up the phone and started walking toward the back of the class

That also happened to be where I was sitting.

Her flats clacked against the tile floor, echoing in the silent room. All of the pencils had paused as everyone tuned their ears toward her and whoever she was heading toward.

She stopped short at the desk belonging to the boy who was sitting in front of me.

He was an ordinary kid, all things considered. Not very talkative in class, but he always knew the right answers to the questions. He and I had only spoken a few times.

His name was Derrick, I think. Derrick Bauer.

He had shaggy blond hair that was even more blond lately from being out in the sun. The back of his neck and forearms were tan, too. Made me wonder if he liked to fish. Or was a farmer. Maybe he just liked to play football outside with his buddies. He was cute enough and was always nice to me.

Miss Patterson knelt down beside his seat.

I pretended to be really stuck on this last problem, my pencil hovering over the equation that I knew was wrong, but my ears strained to hear what she was saying.

"Hey, Derrick. That was the office, saying that your dad was here to—"

"Wait, my dad?" he asked. There was a slight note of panic in his voice. "He's not supposed to be here. He doesn't have custody. He can't check me out of school—"

Miss Patterson was nodding her head. "I know, I know. That's what they told me. The principal is talking with him right now, letting him know that legally, we cannot release you to him if he isn't your designated pick-up that we have on file. I know your mom changed that recently, but the school would be liable if you were to go home with him."

I saw Derrick's shoulders tense. "All right."

Miss Patterson nodded and patted his shoulder gently. "I just wanted you to know what was going on."

"Thanks," Derrick said, returning his eyes to his quiz.

Yeah, right. I'd give up right then and there, if I were him. There'd be no room in my head for concentrating anymore on math.

Normal fell back over the room for a few minutes as pencils scratched across their papers and a frustrated groan came from one kid near the door who I was pretty sure was failing anyways.

Even I got distracted, trying to figure out why I couldn't get my problem to come out right before we were all roused from our stupors when the voice of the principal came over the intercom.

"Initiating lockdown procedures. Initiating lockdown procedures. This is not a drill."

The entire room seemed to freeze over. Even Miss Patterson, who'd returned to her desk, turned and stared up at the speaker. It was like the whole room was an exhibit at Madam Tussauds, everyone made of wax but oh so lifelike.

"Initiating lockdown procedures. Initiating lockdown procedures. This is not a drill."

Lockdown. This is not a drill.

Wait.

"Lock the door," I heard myself say. I was standing, somehow, pointing at the door. When did that happen?

No one was moving. My vision was tunneling. Everything was happening all at once and not at all.

"Miss Patterson," I said in a firm tone. "You need to lock the door. Now."

The principal's voice came back over the intercom.

"All students and staff, please report to the nearest classroom or office. Remain there until further notice. Ensure doors are locked and stay away from all windows and doors."

He was speaking hastily, which made it even worse. My blood was pounding in my ears and I was ready to run.

"Do not open your doors for anyone that you do not recognize or does not have a visitor's pass."

There was an intruder?

All the color left my face as I gripped my pencil. A motion out in the hall caught my eye, drawing my gaze to the window in the door that looked out of the room.

There was a man, a very large, broad shouldered man, striding down the hall with purpose. He had a wild look in his eyes, his teeth were grit. He had an angular head with wild, long salt and pepper hair that looked like it hadn't been washed in weeks, a long nose and ears that were almost perked up.

My blood ran cold. It didn't look like he was carrying anything in his hands, but it didn't matter. He was looking for something.

Or someone.

"Miss Patterson," I said from my desk. "Lock the door. Now!"

Miss Patterson seemed to come to and as she stood, her hands trembling. "Get away from the windows, and just stay quiet." She hurried to the door, locked it, turned out the lights and then rushed back to her desk.

The room was dark and silent. No one moved. No one even dared to breathe.

The footsteps from the man out in the hall grew closer and closer. He was shouting something. I couldn't hear him clearly, but it was making every nerve in my body feel like it was on fire.

I crawled down onto the floor, between the back wall and the bookshelves, shielding me from the doorway. My heart hammered against my chest.

We were trapped in this classroom with nothing but a flimsy lock to separate us from some lunatic who was stalking through the school. I'd been through vampire attacks, assaults from witches and wizards, a faerie war. But a human coming in to attack us? Why was this so frightening to me?

"Oh my God…"

I looked over and realized that it was Derrick who crawled up beside me along the wall. He was peering out around the corner of the bookshelf, staring up at the window in the door. His mouth was hanging slightly open as he leaned back out of sight.

"It's…it's my dad."

Chapter 2

"Holy crap. Holy crap, holy crap, *holy crap!*"

I could hear the whispers of the other kids in the classroom. Some were hiding along the wall that the door was on, beside bookshelves and tables. Some girl was whimpering on the other side of the room, followed by a chorus of "shush!" from other students.

Derrick was rubbing his hands over his face, muttering to himself under his breath.

I didn't want to tell him that I'd overheard the conversation he had with Miss Patterson, but it was obvious that this kid's dad was just a psychopath. What did he do in the office? Did he threaten someone? Did he have a weapon? Were we going to end up on the national news by the end of the day?

I jumped as a loud banging filled the room.

Derrick's dad was at the door, banging as hard as he could against the heavy metal.

"Derrick? Derrick, I know you're in there."

As one, all of the eyes in the classroom shifted toward the corner where Derrick and I were holed up.

An uncomfortable, prickly sensation passed over me, as if everyone was ready to grab him and toss him out to alleviate the tension in the room.

"You need to come with me, son. It's very important," Derrick's dad said, giving the door another few bangs.

I heard one girl burst into tears on the other side of the room.

It didn't really surprise me that some of the students were having actual panic attacks. These sorts of situations were only things we heard about in the news, or on social media. No one ever really thought that they'd end up like this, staring the depravity of humans in the face.

I chewed on my lip as I tried to figure out what to do.

Derrick was trembling beside me, his hands over his head. I couldn't really blame him. This was probably the scariest thing that he'd gone through in his entire life. It was probably the worst thing that any of these kids had dealt with.

The worst part for him, though, was that it was his dad.

I was calloused. I'd been in danger so much that I was starting to become all too familiar with that fickle fight or flight reaction that I'd learned so much about in psychology class. It coursed through me like an old, familiar friend. I was probably going to develop an ulcer by the time I was twenty with how much of my life I spent stressed out so much I wanted to be sick.

Everything that I had been through…everything I had suffered, fought for, learned, experienced…it all felt like fantasy up to this point.

But this was the real world. This was happening in my school, filled with humans, to a human kid who was just terrified of his dad. It was a harsh reality for me to remember that people, normal people, not supernatural creatures, could be scumbags, too.

Was there nowhere that was safe? Did every inch of the earth seethe with disgusting, vile, selfish nature?

I shook my head. Now was not the time to go into an existential shock.

The pounding on the door made me jump again.

"Derrick, this is the last time. I will break this door down—"

"No," Derrick shouted and a few other cries were heard around the room, anticipating an attack or a more direct threat. "No, Dad. I'm not coming with you."

All I could hear was the blood rushing in my ears as we waited for the reply. I really was expecting the door to come crashing down, somehow and then wondered what in the world I was going to have to do in order to get out of the situation, along with everybody else.

We were on the first floor. Was there any way that we could somehow make it to the windows, crawl out and be in the clear before he broke the door down?

"Derrick, you listen here," his dad said. "I'm here to give you your legacy. It's time. Now, open this door!" His last three words were matched with pounding against the metal door.

I looked over at Derrick, who was breathing hard.

"Don't," I whispered.

He looked over at me.

I just shook my head. If he was anything like me, he was considering facing his dad. Of getting up and dealing with it. But it was stupidly unwise.

It looked like I was about to play the part of Iona for a few minutes. If that's what it came to, then I was ready for it.

"But he already knows I'm here," Derrick whispered.

I pressed my finger to my lips. Just because he knew the truth, it didn't mean that Derrick had to give himself up so easily.

There had been a minute or so without any banging. I chanced a look around the corner of the shelf. I could see Derrick shaking his head out of the corner of my eye, telling me to stop, just like I'd told him not to.

But his dad was still there, standing out in the hall. He was staring all around the frame of the door, as if he were missing something. Wondering if there was some way that he could unlock the door from the outside.

Suddenly, Derrick's dad stiffened. His whole body went rigid and he turned his head as if someone had called out to him.

I watched him, holding my breath.

He turned back around, his eyes narrowed. He gave the door one last desperate look over.

And then he stalked away.

"What's happening?" Derrick asked, his voice trembling. "Why do you have that look on your face?"

I shook my head. I still didn't think it was wise to speak. Did he leave to go find something to break the door down with? If he did manage that, would we have the right sort of protection inside the room?

Miss Patterson's desk wasn't all that far from the door. If we hurried and a few of us helped, we could probably shove it in front of the door. And if we managed to cover the window, too, somehow –

"Sirens!"

I looked over and saw Derrick's face lighting up as he sat up straight, staring out toward the windows.

"The police are here!" I heard another girl shriek.

"Oh, thank God!" called another.

I saw the silhouette of Miss Patterson stagger to her feet; she'd been behind her desk the whole time. She looked like a deer caught in the headlights.

"Are we safe?" asked another girl.

"I don't know," said the boy next to her.

There was a beep as the principal's voice came back over the intercom.

"Attention students and staff. Please remain in your rooms. The police have arrived and are going to proceed to search each room. We ask that you remain patient as we resolve this situation."

Miss Patterson collapsed into her chair at her desk, having lost the strength to stand.

Other students were crowding together, already chittering like little birds, talking over one another in one corner of the room.

I pulled myself up to my feet and wobbled over to my desk. My legs were like jelly. I wasn't sure they would hold me. I sank down onto my chair, my tailbone striking the hard plastic, but I slid right out onto the floor.

Everything was shaking. My head was swimming. I felt like I was ready to puke.

I had been through a lot since moving to Florida. I had dealt with violence, death and close calls. I'd been hurt, badly at times. I had walked into a room filled with vampires, sure that it was going to end in my death.

But this…this was something way more real than vampires or faeries.

Chapter 3

Who hadn't learned to fear school shootings over the last few years?

The stunning imagery of running children, the raw gut-punch feeling of knowing kids had been targeted – again, the sheer, clenching fear as we watch it play out on the news networks for endless days after the incident.

The twisted parts of my mind always wondered what it would be like to live through something like that. To experience a real lockdown in the school because of a dangerous person. The human mind relishes torment. That's why we all watch horror movies with jump scares and gore, tickling parts of our brain designed to warn us of a snake in the brush or an enemy hiding in the woods.

Maybe movies were easier because we know they aren't real. We can turn off the television or shut off our phones or walk, knees clacking together, out of the theater and know that our lives will never be the nightmares that the actors pretend to go through.

Living through the lockdown, though?

It wasn't anything like I thought it would be.

No one tells you how cold the room gets, or how chills rack your spine as you try to reassure yourself that the school isn't an unsafe place and that yes, you'll be able to come back. Tomorrow, even, in our case.

They don't mention how time slows down as you wonder about yourself and your own safety and they definitely don't say anything about the guilt that follows after you realize you're fine.

He didn't have a gun, but the fear, the uncertainty, held a power over us, nonetheless, lingering long after he was gone. It was as though he'd tripped some primal trigger within us, primed to be hit at any moment.

Girls held onto one another in the parking lot after we'd been evacuated, makeup smeared under their eyes from glittering tears. The guys stood together in solidarity, eyes distant and faces blank.

I'd faced worse than this. Much worse.

Even still…the atmosphere that surrounded me was almost funereal. You couldn't get this many members of the student body together and expect this much of a quiet pall to fall over them. Assemblies were loud and raucous.

This was dead…as if somebody had actually died.

At least no one had. That would've been enough to ruin everyone's month.

News spread fast in these kinds of situations. Even though we'd been told to not contact anyone on the outside of the school until everything had been sorted out, parents still showed up, waiting behind the police line, their faces stricken, as though expecting casualties to be announced in spite of the all clear having been given.

I watched it all through the window of our classroom, wondering how everyone else was feeling. Since our room was the one that had been impacted, they took extra time to question each of us. We told them that Derrick's dad was long gone; he'd taken off before they even showed up. Derrick's face was as pale as a vampire's as they led him from the room for questioning. I couldn't imagine how he must've been feeling.

Poor kid.

When they finally let us out, I walked past a group of girls just outside the front doors who were two years younger than me, all of them on their cell phones.

"Oh my gosh, you guys, I am literally shaking," said one girl with more makeup on than I had ever worn in my life.

"I've never been more scared," her friend said, clutching her face in her hands.

"This is the most traumatic thing to ever happen in my life," the third said. "I need to see my therapist, like, immediately."

Before moving to Florida, I probably would've been traumatized like them, if they actually were going to take it as more than a chance to get attention on social media. They were certainly all well set to get their fifteen minutes of fame today.

My legs and back ached, the adrenaline leaving a painful reminder in every nerve that I had been in life or death, fight or flight stress. Again. My head throbbed and I knew that I desperately needed quiet. Which was unlikely to happen with the entire student body clumped in great globs on the front lawn, hemmed in like cattle by yellow police tape.

"Hey, Cassie!" It was Xandra, waving at me from one of the picnic tables alongside the school.

I wandered over, grabbing a crisis blanket from an unattended ambulance as I passed. I offered it to her as I approached.

"Girl, I'm fine, do you not feel how hot it is? You could fry an egg on the sidewalk," she said, waving a hand dismissively. "I saw those freshmen gawking at you."

I rolled my eyes and looked back at the social media trio I'd passed on the way out. They hurriedly went back to their phones from admiring me. "What's that all about?"

"You look cooler than most right now." Xandra winked at me. "Not your first rodeo, right?"

"So, are your parents here?" I asked her, changing the subject as quickly as I could. "I assume after everything they've dealt with lately…" I trailed off, giving her a pointed look.

She shook her head. "Nah. I texted them and told them what happened. But this isn't the first time something like this has happened. Lots of parents try to come and pick up their kids without legal permission." She looked at me with a steady gaze. "That's what happened, right? At least that's the rumor going around."

"Yeah, it is," I said. "Dad gone mad. He was trying to pick up a kid in my class."

"The rumor mill got it right this time," she said, nodding. She was playing with the black choker necklace she was wearing. "Who'd-a thunk it? How about you? Is your mom in complete freak out mode?"

"I texted them too," I said. "I said, *I'm okay, don't panic.*" I shrugged. "I've ignored the twenty-seven follow-up texts. They would *know* if anything was wrong. But Mom's gonna mom."

Xandra gave me an understanding nod. "Yep. That's true."

There was a group of police officers off to the side, crowding around in a circle. I could just make out Derrick's blond hair through the wall of navy uniforms.

"He's such a normal kid," Xandra said, following my gaze. "Like, good grades, never goes to parties. Sweet sort of guy. I guess there's weirdos in every family."

"Does that make me the weirdo in mine?" I asked.

"Probably. You don't really have any competition and your boyfriend drinks blood, so..."

"Very good points in my favor." I nodded along, then fell into a pensive state listening to a single siren whooping in the distance, some cop who hadn't shut off the noise on his car when he parked. I'd seen a side of Derrick that maybe nobody ever had before.

He had been *terrified* of his dad. Not angry, not excited.

Terrified.

That raised a lot of questions in my mind. Was Derrick so quiet because he was dealing with abuse at home? Did he put on a good face here because he was hiding what was going on in his life outside of school?

The police circle around him started to break, officers wandering off in ones and twos. Two of them hung back about ten feet from him as the others headed off, on guard duty, apparently. They looked serious, talking in low voices just outside his earshot.

Derrick just stood there, all by himself, looking lost like a wallflower on prom night.

"Did you open this yet?" I asked Xandra, eyeing a water bottle on the table.

"No, they brought 'em around when they offered us

13

blankets," Xandra said. "This being Florida, I get the water bottles. Still wondering about the blankets. At ninety-two degrees, it just defies logic."

I scooped the bottle off the table and started back across the parking lot.

"Don't forget to text Mill," she shouted after me, teasing me. "You know how he worries."

She really liked to have the last jab, didn't she?

Derrick was standing underneath a live oak tree, with sprawling branches overhead that I would have loved to have climbed if I were a kid. He had a crisis blanket in his arms and was staring at his feet. He was about a head taller than me, but by his posture and the slump of his shoulders, you would have thought he was two feet tall. He didn't see me coming.

"Hey," I said in a quiet, easy tone, trying not to spook him.

He looked up and to my surprise, he gave me a small smile. I guess there wasn't going to be much that would scare him after what we had just gone through. "Hey," he said.

I held out the water bottle to him. "Here."

"Thanks," he said, taking it. This close, I saw that his eyes were the same color as the sky in winter, a cool, pale blue that was haloed in green. He glanced over my shoulder as he unscrewed the cap and I followed his gaze. The teachers and principal were speaking with the police officers who'd just been surrounding Derrick.

"They're trying to decide what to do with me," he said, his expression not changing.

I looked back at him. "What do you mean?"

His eyes fell. "Well, it's my fault that this happened in the first place, you know? If it wasn't for my dad—"

"It's not your fault," I said, shaking my head. "It's not like you told your dad to storm the school."

Derrick didn't reply; the guilt was still clear on his face. He just exhaled heavily through his nose, then took a long sip from the water bottle.

"I'll take your silence as a yes," I said.

He just read the label of the water bottle; *Pure spring water bottled at the source.*

"Your mom's not here yet, I guess?" I asked, looking

around.

He shook his head. "No."

"I see," I said.

An even more awkward silence fell over us and some birds sang to one another in the tree over our head.

"Well, I won't bother you for long," I said. "I just wanted to make sure that you were okay." I turned to head back toward Xandra, when Derrick spoke up again.

"I'm sorry. It's Cassie, right?"

I stopped and glanced at him over my shoulder. "Yeah."

He stared down at his brand new blue Nike sneakers. "I'm sorry if my dad freaked you out."

I tilted my head to the side, surveying him. This kid really had a guilt complex, didn't he?

"Why would you be sorry about that?" I asked. "I already told you, it's not—"

"I know, it's not my fault. But I could have handled myself better. I...just kind of freaked out."

I shook my head. "It was your dad. We don't expect our parents to be anything other than perfect, do we?"

He looked down at me with wide eyes. "Uhm..."

"I learned the hard way that my parents are just people. Normal people with normal fears and mostly normal wants, except for my dad's weird thing with collecting old, unopened baseball cards. He gets them, then opens, then chews the gum, even though it's hard as a piece of wood. I really don't know what's going on with that. It's gotta taste like old cardboard-"

"Parents aren't perfect, no," Derrick said, oh-so-politely, knocking me back on track.

"Right," I said. "They just happen to be older and are in charge of taking care of us. It's hard being an adult. With bills and...stuff." Whatever adults did. Watched cable instead of Netflix and Hulu, I assume. Suffered through commercials trying to sell them old-age creams and insurance.

"Yeah, I hear that," he said, his eyebrows disappearing underneath his hair as he nodded. "I've learned a lot these last couple years just how childish my parents are. How petty they can be."

I could almost feel a life story coming on. I might as well

have had *counselor* tattooed on my forehead.

"My mom is divorcing my dad," Derrick said, eyes back on his shoelaces. "It's been really messy for weeks now. Months really."

Ouch, divorce. Thankfully, that wasn't something that I had to deal with in my own family, but I'd had friends that went through it. Still, I had no idea what to tell Derrick. What do you say to someone whose whole world felt like it was falling apart?

It struck me that I did sort of know what that was like. Not divorce, but threat of death and my parents being kidnapped all sort of drew out similar sorts of feelings, didn't it? Paralyzing fear, inability to think of anything else, desperate attempts to fix everything...

"In my own way, I get what you're feeling right now," I said. "I've been through some pretty rough stuff in my own life."

"Divorce?" he asked.

I shook my head. "No. Not divorce."

"I know this is going to sound stupid, but...I don't think you know it unless you've been through it." He hung his head. "He's my dad, but since this started he's...he's just gone *wild*. He's out of control. Mom and I don't really know what's going on with him."

"When did all this start?"

"I don't know." A shrug ran heavy all along Derrick's shoulders, making him seem like a scarecrow torn loose by strong wind. "He's always been kind of a weird guy, but lately, it's been worse. Like, as the years went on, his temper got worse. He takes his anger out on Mom. He and I got into a fight about something once, like a physical fight. And the next day, it was like he didn't remember it. Or maybe didn't want to. He's moody on and off and I can't ever tell if he is going to be my dad like he used to or...I dunno. Mr. Hyde, maybe."

Jekyll/Hyde? That sounded like a psychological break, honestly. "What does your dad do?" I asked.

"He's kind of a freelancer," Derrick said with a shrug. "He does odd jobs. Plumbing, electrical, landscaping. He is never happy anywhere for very long. Changes employers a lot." He sighed heavily. "I don't get it. He takes his frustrations out on us because we're all he has. But...I've never seen him do anything like he did today."

"What do his outbursts look like?" I asked. I wasn't really sure why I was asking, other than maybe my gentle probing was helping him talk about it and earning me that forehead *Counselor* tattoo.

Yeah, right. It's actually because I was a magnet for the bizarre and unnatural.

"He disappears for days at a time," Derrick said. "Mom thinks he goes to drink himself into oblivion. He comes home, stumbling in, bloody, looking like he was in some sort of fight."

Gone for days at a time, looking worse for wear when coming home. Angry, aggressive. Snarling at the door like some sort of...animal.

The sirens in my mind went off full blast.

Mood changes, shoddy memory, coming home looking like he'd been in a fight.

Then today, charging into the school and stalking his son like he was prey. Derrick even used the word *wild* when describing him.

"Sorry, I don't really know why I told you all that," Derrick said, rubbing the back of his neck. "I guess I haven't really told anyone."

"It's cool," I said. "I get it. Everyone is only pretending their life is perfect. Beneath the surface, every smoothly swimming swan is paddling like mad."

"Hah." He gave me a grateful ghost of a smile. "Thanks. I'm glad you aren't upset with me. Though I probably looked like a coward, huddled in that corner of the room. I should've faced him."

"What good would it have done?" I asked. "You aren't a coward. It was smart."

"I don't know about that." He lifted the empty water bottle. "Thanks."

"Yeah, no problem," I said and then turned to walk away.

But before I got very far, I hesitated.

Stay out of it, a little voice chimed in, talking in the back of my head. Don't ask, don't ask —

17

"Hey, Derrick?" I asked, turning back around.

"Yeah?"

"Your dad…he wasn't…" I felt a real squeeze in my guts, pressure from trying to get this out, but out it popped anyway, "…by any chance…Amish, in the past?"

He blinked, giving me a funny look. "Yeah, he was. He left his community when he turned eighteen. How – how did you know that?"

Crap.

"Oh, just a guess," I said, forcing a smile. "I…know some Amish. Sort of."

Derrick gave me a curious look. "No one has ever guessed that before. Wow."

"Well, I'll see you later," I said, not wanting to answer any more questions. "Take care of yourself, all right?"

"All…right," he said. "Bye?"

A lump formed in my throat. I heard Xandra calling to me, but I ignored her. So not in the mood for telling her now.

Of course. I really was a magnet for the weird. That was just the way that my luck ran lately. I should play the lottery – if there was a paranormal Russian roulette lottery that didn't result in the prize of a silver bullet in the skull. Mostly because I'd need that silver bullet, it was sounding like.

Derrick's dad was a werewolf.

Chapter 4

"...And then he takes off running down the hall. I think he heard the police sirens."

I was sitting on Mill's couch next to him, feeling like it was the dead of night even though it was only six p.m. His windows were all sealed from the sun, but he kept the place well-lit and comfortable. Still, the lack of natural light gave it a forever-night sort of feel.

Masculine highlighted the leathers and wood finishes, but he'd started to give the place a little softer touch as of late. He always had fresh flowers in a vase where I tossed my keys and phone and he kept his fridge stocked with my favorite soda and snacks. I noticed that he'd started to keep enough food for actual meals, too, his fridge no longer floor-to-ceiling blood packs from the local Red Cross. He was getting to be a pretty good cook, too, considering he hadn't needed to eat real food in years.

He was sipping from a stainless steel tumbler, freshly awake. I appreciated the fact that he never used clear mugs around me. I could just pretend that he was drinking coffee, because it looked like he was. I just didn't look too closely at the lip of the lid for fear of fixating on the crimson residue that gathered around the sipping hole.

"So, you're convinced that this guy is a werewolf?" Mill set his cup down on the coffee table. He was so graceful it didn't even clatter on the clear glass.

"Pretty much," I said. "I mean, it adds up, doesn't it? He has mood swings that are inconsistent but keep happening. Could be the full moon, right? He disappears for days at a time. Probably transforming and then coming back after. And he was Amish, Mill. I mean, I know they aren't all werewolves, but he lives in Florida and there's a werewolf clan among the Amish down in Sarasota. I'm drawing a line here and it's a pretty straight one for me. He looks like a werewolf."

"That's a lot of speculation," Mill said.

"But you should've seen him," I said, shaking my head. "He looked vicious. His teeth were all bared, shoulders hunched, as he was stalking down the hall. I didn't spend all that much time with the werewolves, but they sort of moved the same." I tapped my chin. "But the Amish were all in control of themselves. This guy…he was totally different."

"Yeah, because there's a huge difference between Amish werewolves and the ones who aren't in the order," Mill said. "But I guess you wouldn't know that, would you?"

"Okay, what's the matter with you?" I asked, sitting up, glaring at him. "You're usually grumpy when I wake you up early, but this is something else. Have I offended thee, somehow? Did I spit in your blood, giving it a flavor of Cheetos or something? Do I need to leave so you can unkink your vampire hose?"

He blinked at me. "Vampire hose? Is that slang for goth ladies?"

"No," I said, throwing my arms up. "I said it, realized it didn't really mean anything, so now I kind of want to take it back, like deleting a pic on Instaphoto that you shouldn't have posted."

"I know I'm kinda old compared to you, but I'm pretty sure spoken words don't work like that," he said. "And no, you didn't do anything wrong."

"Did my traumatic day inconvenience you, then?" I asked.

"Of course not," he said. "It's just a shame that the police didn't shoot that guy down like the dog he is right outside the school."

I could almost hear the seconds tick by as I stared at him, dumbfounded. My mouth fell open and I floundered around for words.

Had I heard him right? I couldn't have. There's no way. He didn't…really think that…did he?

"Um…what?" I asked.

Mill didn't flinch. "I hate werewolves."

I laughed hollowly. "You're joking, right? Werewolves…they helped you, Mill. Helped me. They were wonderful. How can you say that?" I stared him down. "Are you so up your own ass that you can't get off *Team Edward* for a second and see that the werewolves here have done some real good?"

Mill sighed, shaking his head. "I'll tell you what's wrong with werewolves." He sat up a little more. "They're hairy. Mean. Ugly. Their breath is terrible. They bite, they scratch, they use their claws. It's never a fair fight with a werewolf."

"And vampires don't use their teeth?" I asked incredulously.

"That's different," Mill said. "We only use our teeth when we intend to drain someone. Anything else…well, it's just savage."

"And drinking blood isn't?" I pointed at his tumbler.

"Vampires at least go about their killing with some class," Mill said. "Werewolves have none. They're no better than beasts."

"Wow." I stood up and started pacing. I didn't want to sit next to him anymore. "I didn't realize that your dislike of werewolves was all petty surface stuff," I said. "I was sure that you of all people would be able to give me some sort of deep, philosophical argument, but it's really down to, 'Eww, gross doggo mean.'"

"They really are." Mill shrugged. "And I hate 'em."

"You know, I expected better of you," I said. "You're so nonchalant about your anti-werewolf bigotry."

"It's not bigotry," Mill said. "Bigotry is ill-informed prejudice based on something like misunderstanding or fear of the unknown. I know exactly what I despise about werewolves and if you get into a fight with one of them and lose your lower intestine for a few days you'll hate them, too."

It was making my blood boil how casually he was saying this stuff. "I don't think that you can make an assumption about the entire species based on the actions of a few or one,

21

Millard."

He winced. "I should not have told you my full name."

"Do you even hear yourself?" I asked. "I really don't like this side of you. Your 1800's upbringing is showing."

"I get that you always want to see the best in others," Mill said, "but I'm sorry that I don't share your modernist, flowery view of the world. I thought that, by now, you'd see that not everything is rainbows and sunshine. This isn't about nearly-intangible differences like race or sexuality, things that have no bearing on a person. Paranormal creatures are separated from humans by a wide gulf and it's nothing to do with appearances. You've seen just how terrible vampires are. How *most* vampires are. Iona and I are rare birds. You know that, right?"

I shook my head. I couldn't believe what I was hearing.

"I'm not trying to upset you," Mill said. "But sometimes I think you forget that vampires are monsters. Well, werewolves are, too. And so much worse than the two of us."

"Look, Mill, this kid is going through a really rough time," I said, aware that I was definitely ignoring that last thought. "His dad is going through a rough spot, too. People are deeper than what they show on the outside."

"Sometimes," he said, nodding his head. "But that doesn't automatically mean that I'm to like what I find underneath. Maybe his rough exterior is hiding something even worse. Something that's bubbling up after being held down for a nice, long while."

I grimaced.

"You hope that there's good in everyone and I totally understand and appreciate that," he said. "But you have not lived as long as I have, Cassie. You haven't seen just how wretched the world is and how the good people are fewer and farther between than any of us would like. Especially when they've been altered by the paranormal." He shook his head. "Power like that which comes from vampires, werewolves...it corrupts. In unpredictable ways."

"You're corrupted?" I asked. "I'm not having a hard time believing that, at least not after this conversation."

"I don't think I'm really getting through here," he said, a

pinched look on his face. "Maybe we should just agree to disagree about werewolves."

"You think just because you've been living a long time you get to have a sour opinion of the world?" I asked.

"Sour's a bridge too far. No, I think it's a realistic opinion," he said. "Most people, super-natural creatures included, are out for themselves. When you sprinkle power imbalances into that equation, it leads to violence and suffering. I think good intentions are only skin deep most of the time – and only held at bay by threat of reprisal."

"Wow," I said. "What a sad world you live in. It's so bleak. How do you get out of bed in the morning?"

"I have you," he said plainly, without missing a beat.

My cheeks burned bright red, but I turned away. If he was trying to flatter me in order to distract me, it wasn't going to work. "When we ran into trouble with Draven, Iona went straight to the Amish werewolves," I said, trying to stay up on my high horse. "She didn't have an issue with them."

"Iona is her own breed of crazy," Mill said. "But I understand why she went there."

I blinked at him. "Wait, what? You don't like them, but you understand going to them for help?"

"The Amish are different than other werewolves," Mill said. "They act as a group, keep each other accountable. They have self-discipline because they have faith in a power higher than themselves. Rogue werewolves, those without a pack, are narcissistic, shallow creatures and often vicious. They have no constraints or boundaries to keep themselves in check and usually no one around to help them. They truly give in to the wild beast within themselves and live only to maim, kill and slaughter. There is no higher calling to hold them back. No fear of reprisal. After all...who would stop them?"

"It sounds so hopeless," I said.

"That's because it is," Mill said. "If they aren't kept on a leash, especially the young ones, there would be a lot more wanton violence in the world around us."

"You don't think that any werewolf outside of a pack couldn't reform himself? Keep himself in check?" I asked.

Mill shook his head. "Do you think a vampire without any

guidance could choose not to murder every human that walked across their path?"

"I can't deal with this right now," I said, shaking my head. I snatched up my keys, my cell phone and backpack from the entryway. I totally ignored the roses in the vase. "All I wanted was your support and you're just sitting there cutting me down, hopes and attitude first." I turned and stared at him.

"You're leaving already?" He hadn't moved from the couch.

"It's a little too dark in here for me and I don't mean the lack of sunlight or your over-reliance on CFL bulbs," I said, my heartbeat throbbing against my eardrums. "My parents have sent me about three hundred and eighteen text messages. This—" I said, motioning to the distance between us, "To be continued. I – I hate myself for even sinking to this low, teenager-ish level, but...I just can't even with you right now."

"Come on, Cassie," Mill said, getting to his feet. "I'm sorry."

"For what?"

"Upsetting you," he said, taking it slow as he crossed to me rather than whizzing over at full vampire speed, which would probably just freak me out.

"But you aren't sorry for what you said, are you?" I asked, slinging my backpack over my shoulder.

"No," Mill said. "I'm not. I sort of wish that you hadn't met the Amish werewolves. They've severely skewed your impression of their kind."

"'Their kind'?" I asked, moving closer to the door. "Are you freaking serious with this, Millard?"

"Seriously, stop saying my full name like that. You're not my mother." He blinked twice, perhaps reconsidering what he'd just said. "Fortunately. On so many levels."

I rolled my eyes. "Ugh. Mill." I reached the door, threw it open and turned around, shooting him a glare. "Let me introduce you to another thing that my generation does that yours probably never did. A storm out."

And I slammed the door behind me.

I could hear him inside, probably because he raised his voice. "No, we did that."

Chapter 5

My phone screen lit up. I noticed it out of the corner of my eye, but I ignored it for a second. I needed to figure out this stupid problem.

I was sitting cross-legged on my bed, poring over my math book. It was almost eight o'clock and I had just started my homework. Normally, I was done by now, but with everything that had happened today I was way behind and camped out on my rented bed in our rented house.

I'd had the inevitable conversation with Mom and Dad when I got home. It went about as well as you might expect.

"There weren't any vampires involved, right?" Mom asked, a thousand times.

I assured her that no, no vampires were involved. It was a totally normal, non-vampire event. Not that these things really were normal. Thankfully. If you went a thousand days at a thousand schools, you would almost never see anything quite as dramatic as this happen. But the moment you did, it was burned indelibly into your memory, forever coloring your feelings about the probability of such an event.

Also, cable news pumped these things out to everyone like visual crack. Anything that hit kids was like a perfect horror movie for parents. They couldn't tear themselves away from that slow, mortifying build of revulsion and fear.

"But that boy was in your class?" Dad had asked, shaking his head like he couldn't wrap it around what was going on. "Why do all of these things happen to you?"

If only he knew how often I asked myself that question. They asked me probably a thousand more before we had finished and I'd finally been able to tackle my homework. I had escaped without having to answer that one, because it would have gone something like, "Because I lied so much in New York that I forced us to move to the middle of Vampire Town, USA."

In the realm of strategic lies, I had also neglected to mention the fact that a werewolf was involved in today's incident. I know, I know. A lie of omission. But hey, I was getting better, right? Rome wasn't built in a day and all that.

I finished my problem and checked my phone to find what looked like Xandra just mashing random buttons on the text screen before sending it.

Stressed much? I sent as a reply.

Number twelve. I am going to pull all my hair out, she'd written. *All of it. Every beautiful blue-ish strand. I'm going to look like Ripley from Alien 3, or that one weirdo on the album my parents have. Sinead O something or another. Maybe I'll join a nunnery.*

Another text, a moment later: *Nuns don't have to do math, do they?*

They'd probably take a dim view of the blue hair if you decided to grow it back and dye it at some point, I texted back. *That problem is where I am.*

Shaving your head and joining a nunnery is where you're at, too? And I thought after all these months of vampires you had better coping mechanisms than that.

I found myself beset by a case of the giggles at her text. I replied: *I can't even believe that they didn't just cancel homework and tests for the rest of the year. Why can't Dumbledore be our headmaster?*

I think we'd be in a lot more trouble if Voldemort was waiting at the end of this, she replied. *Besides, you already bested your dark lord a month ago. We should be in for clear sailing. Instead we get this crap. I declare shenanigans.*

Go ahead. See what declaring shenanigans gets you. I'm guessing it'll be a zero on your homework, because a declaration of shenanigans isn't a finished assignment. I smiled and put aside my phone, struggling with the problem for a few more minutes until she sent me another message.

So when are you going to tell me what you talked about with Derrick?

I groaned. I really didn't feel like talking about it, especially after the conversation with Mill, but I knew she was going to bug me for pretty much the rest of my life and it was easier to text it to her than to answer her questions in person, where there was a chance to be overheard. I settled in and typed it all out as quickly as I could, throwing in a requisite amount of u's in place of "you" and b's in place of "be" because I'm a teenager and that's a huge timesaver.

So what does that mean for this whole situation? she asked once I was done with my thumb-killing explanation.

Means I hope he doesn't show up at the full moon? I sent back.

Ha, ha. But seriously. Do you think Derrick knows?

I don't think so, I sent. *He seemed surprised I guessed he'd been Amish when he was younger.*

Oh! One of those wily few who actually leaves the community, huh? Interesting, Xandra texted back. *Permanent Rumspringa!*

It does make me wonder if Derrick is a werewolf, too, I sent back. *I mean, his dad said something about "giving him his legacy" today when he was ranting and raving through the door,* I said.

Do you think he's just completely wacko? she asked.

I rule nothing out. Mill said that werewolves who are not a part of a pack are like wild animals, I texted her. Even if I was angry with Mill, now that I was removed from him, I could sort of pick through what he said and look at it more logically. *So, I guess, in a way, yeah. He might be completely wacko.*

It's so weird that there are just so many super-natural beings around us and we just totally had no clue, she texted me.

You said it, girl. You said it.

So why did he make a scene over Derrick? she asked. *That legacy thing?*

Whatever that might be, I said. *Derrick seemed to think it had something to do with his parents' divorce.*

I heard the doorbell downstairs and my ears perked up. That was odd. It was after eight. Who would be here this late?

Could've been our neighbor, telling Dad that he left the grill on. Or maybe it was postal guys, dropping off a package from Amazon. I racked my brain – did I order anything in the last few days? No, but that didn't matter, my mom was forever ordering stuff.

"Cassie?"

Dad's voice carried down the hall from the tiny kitchen.

"What?" I shouted back, slamming my math book shut. To hell with it. If my teacher couldn't spare any mercy for my not finishing this stupid problem after today, I'd take the incomplete and try harder next time, when I was more well-rested and less emotionally drained.

"There's a boy here to see you," my dad called back.

My eyes narrowed. A boy?

My heart rose as I thought of Mill, wondering if maybe he had come over to work things out, which was quickly followed by a flare of resentment that he hadn't done that yet.

But no. If it was Mill, Dad would have said so.

I opened the door to my room, padding out into the carpeted living area in my bare feet, silently wishing my dad had gone for vague and it really was Mill, here with a fresh dozen roses and a grand gesture of apology. A Whitman's sampler wouldn't go unnoticed, especially after today.

When I got to the door, though...it definitely wasn't Mill. Not even close.

Out on the front step of the rental house, framed by the porch light and shivering in the darkness was the bespectacled face of Gregory Holt, my once and future neighbor and the nerdiest dude I knew. And by the look he was giving me...my trying day did not look to be over yet.

Chapter 6

"Can I talk to you alone in your room right now please?" Gregory spat the words out so fast that I wasn't really sure that I had heard him correctly.

His face was pale and his eyebrows one solid, worried line. His Star Trek T-shirt looked like something his mom had bought him when he was in sixth grade and for some reason the very sight of him wearing it, in the state he was in, sapped me of all my anger.

"Um.. hi?" I said, giving him a questioning look. "Let's go back to the beginning. What are you doing here? How did you know we were—"

"Laura told me where your new house was," he said. "Now please, I need to talk to you. It's urgent."

"Sure." I looked over my shoulder at Mom and Dad, both of whom were watching the conversation with arching eyebrows. "If it's okay with my parents?"

Dad sized Gregory up in one up and down sort of look. The scrutiny in his eyes quickly changed to amusement. He glanced over at me and shrugged. No threat there. "Yeah. No problem."

"Okay, good—" Gregory said, stepping in boldly and then stopping like he'd hit an invisible wall of uncertainty. "Uh...where's your room?"

I rolled my eyes and waved him inside, then I closed the door.

He looked like a rat caught in a trap. His eyes were huge and round and he kept looking around nervously. I might have been concerned if I hadn't seen him act this way once before. And that thought didn't really give me any peace about the whole situation, even though I found his ability to spit out words faster than an auctioneer kind of hilarious.

As soon as I led him to my room and closed the door, Gregory wheeled around and pointed a finger at me.

"I—" he said and then he paused, brow furrowing. "Hang on a second. What did your dad mean by that?"

"Nothing?" I said, trying to hide a snort. "I'm sure he was commenting on the fact you look like an upstanding citizen, worthy of trust. Now...what did you need bad enough to track me down and pound on my door tonight?"

Gregory gave me an uncertain look, but shook his head, letting whatever retort was in his mind give way to more important things. "Did you hear about what happened today at school?"

"You mean the crazy guy who came tearing down the halls, shouting and looking for his son, Derrick? That thing?" I asked.

"Duh," Gregory said. "Yeah, that."

"Yeah, dude, I heard about it. I was in the room when it happened."

Gregory's eyes widened and he gasped. "No way! You were? Really?"

"Enhance your calm, Gregory," I said. "Yes, I was in the room. Why?"

"Derrick's a friend of mine," Gregory said. "Close friend. Close-ish friend." He sighed, shaking his head, shifting his weight to his other leg. "Look, we aren't like, besties or anything, but we're close. We play Call of Duty together pretty much every night of the week. Tightest bros of bro-hood."

I was having a really hard time keeping a straight face. I chewed on my bottom lip to keep myself from bursting out laughing. Tightest bros of bro-hood, huh? No wonder my dad didn't find him threatening. "When your bro's birthday?" I folded my arms.

"I don't know and what does that have to do with anything?" Gregory asked, his eyes narrowing behind his glasses.

Ah, yes. Such a typical teenage boy response. Actually, I reflected, thinking about how often my dad forgot his own mother's birthday...maybe it was just a guy thing in general. "Oh, yeah, you guys are super tight. You're practically sharing one of those T-shirts that parents shove their kids into when they aren't getting along," I said with a smirk.

"Listen, my mom made my brother and I wear one of those when we were younger. It ripped so fast that she didn't even bother try getting a new one—" Gregory said.

I did laugh at that, snorted out my nose, in fact.

"It's not funny. My little brother is like the Tasmanian Devil." His face became serious again and I could see the strain behind his eyes. "Cassie...you have to help him. You have to help my bro."

I stared at him. Now it was my turn to be surprised. "Tasmanian Devil one or the one you play video games with?"

"The video g – I mean, Derrick," he said. "You're like...the one who helps people. When things get sticky, you always find a way to get people out of these situations."

I chuckled, but it was mirthless. "You think things work out well when I'm around? Gregory, you've seen my life fall completely to pieces not once, not twice, but at least three times now and you somehow think that I'm good at working these things out?"

"You're still alive, aren't you?" he asked. "And so is everyone you were trying to protect. You've saved my butt, too. Don't think I've forgotten."

And he saved mine once. Which I hadn't forgotten, either.

"Look, Cassie...you just have a better head on your shoulders for this kind of stuff. Maybe it's from your liar past, where you learned to look people in the eye and say whatever to get them to do whatever, all on the fly – whatever the case, you got this in a way no one else our age does. Or older people, either."

"That was an interesting analysis of how my compulsive lying has helped me in life. Not sure I quite see the benefits that way, but...interesting."

"But you know what it's like to be going through a trial like Derrick is," Gregory said. "His parents are in the middle of a

31

really messy divorce. Like, the kind where his mom woke him up in the middle of the night, covered in blood and dragged him out of the house to live somewhere else."

"Whoa." I said.

"Yeah." Gregory nodded. "I've been at his house when his dad gets home. The place just goes quiet except for him the minute he walks in. You can feel the atmosphere change. You ever see fear enter a room just by watching the faces of the people who live there? It's eerie. My skin crawled the first time it happened."

"But he's out now?" I asked. "He and his mom?"

"Yeah," Gregory said, running his hands through his hair nervously. "But I think we all saw today that things are clearly not okay. They're not out of the woods. So...can you help him? Please?"

"You mean help him like I helped Laura?" I asked. "Because I'm starting to get a really strong sense of de ja vu right about now." I folded my arms. "I should start charging for this..."

Gregory shook his head. "No, not like with Laura. Because vampires aren't involved this time." But his face went pale. "Wait, you don't think it's vampires, do you? His dad's not..." He held his first two fingers in front of his mouth.

"Buck-toothed?" I asked, keeping a straight face. "No, his dentistry seemed on point." I chuckled. "No, it's not vamps. Not after we killed about ninety percent of the Tampa clans at Draven's place," I said. "Iona and Mill think the Tampa territory is still unclaimed. And his dad couldn't be a vampire anyways."

"Why not?" Gregory asked, his brow furrowing.

"Sunlight, bro," I said, pointing at the dark window. "He showed up at the school in the middle of the day unprotected."

"Oh," he said. "You're right."

"Is that what you've been thinking all along?" I asked.

"No," he said. "Yes? Maybe?"

I rolled my eyes.

"Cassie, I have no idea. All I know is that things have been super weird in the last, like, six months. I don't know what to expect anymore, or what to rule out. All I know is that my friend is suffering and you somehow have this magical ability to make people's problems go away," Gregory said.

"Gregory, I am not the Godfather," I said. "Or a faerie godmother."

"The way you murder vampires, you sure could have fooled me," he said. "And I'm not asking you to turn a mouse into a carriage horse or make me a new dress."

I gave his Star Trek T-shirt a look. "You sure? Because if I had magic, I'd be all about glamouring those threads into something silky and beautiful rather than...well..." I waved a hand.

"Ouch. You really aren't a faerie godmother, dispensing all fashion criticism and no assistance."

"Look, Gregory, I talked to him a little bit today. He told me basically everything you told me. But I don't see what I can do aside from offering some emotional support. Which you are more capable of doing, being his friend. Or gaming bro. Just hand him a controller and a hill to die on in some virtual foreign battlefield and he should be right as rain in no time. Or as right as he can get given the circumstances."

Gregory hung his head. "Wouldn't it be great if all of life's problems could be fixed like that? By just playing video games and just tuning everything else out?"

His serious tone sort of caught me off guard. "I know what you mean," I said. "And...yes."

Something about the pitying tone rang the bells in my head. I knew what Mill would say before I even finished the thought. No. Big fat no and stay out of it. Just like he did...every time I stuck my nose in the world of the paranormal.

What could I do? I honestly didn't know how to help, especially not with a werewolf's domestic violence situation. Where do you go for that? The cops would be helpless. Would the Amish be able to give some advice? Push me in the right direction? Protect Derrick and his mom from his dad?

Aside from knowing the Amish, I could still probably do more than most. I did have connections. I knew a Faerie, for heaven's sake. And even though I'd definitely leave Mill out of this one, I could get Iona to help, maybe?

The image of Derrick standing under the oak tree that

afternoon flashed across my mind. He looked so consumed in his own thoughts and I'd recognized the haunted expression on his face, having seen it on my own so many times in the mirror.

Would wild werewolves kill their own children? Would Derrick's dad find him before the police captured him? A sick feeling boiled in the pit of my stomach.

Too many questions, too many fears that Derrick was likely dealing with. I could almost feel them for him and I didn't want to reach the bottom of any of them.

If I didn't help...he was helpless and one of those terrible things my mind was racing around might just become reality. My stomach dropped further.

"All right," I said. "I'll see what I can do."

"Thank you, Cassie, thank you so much, " Gregory said, his face visibly relaxing, splitting into a smile. "Seriously, you're the best. What changed your mind?"

"Well," I said, trying to put the words together from the thoughts and feelings that had finally driven me off the fence, "I guess I thought that he shouldn't have to deal with the fact that his dad's a werewolf by himself. Assuming he knows the truth, which I'm not sure he does."

"That's really kind of you, to get involved in this for a stranger like—" Gregory was nodding along happily until what I said finally caught up in his mind and his eyes went wide as his pupils seemed to suck in on themselves. "Wait — did you say *werewolf*?"

Chapter 7

"Hey, Mom."

My mother was in our dining room, staring out of the French doors that led to the backyard. Whenever she sat at the table, she was surrounded by stacks of legal docs, real estate deeds, wills and other important information about people's lives. Her chin in her palm, her eyes narrowed as she stared into the darkness beyond the glass-paned doors, lost in thought.

After a moment her eyes fluttered and she sat up straight. She turned her eyes up to me and smiled. It was tight, distracted. "Hey," she said, taking a deep breath. And that was all, not a breath about Gregory ringing the doorbell and wanting to talk to me in my room alone.

"Scone?" I said. My dad had baked them while I was in with Gregory. I held out the only one that I hadn't already eaten.

"Oh, thanks," she said, taking it. But she just turned it over in her hand and looked out the doors again. After another moment, she stirred. "Is Gregory all right?"

There it was. She seemed to finally remember what was going on around here.

"Yeah, he's fine," I said. "He just had to ask me something about one of his friends. Derrick. He was the kid whose dad…"

"I see," she said, nodding. I couldn't tell if she actually did see or if she was just too lost in thought to formulate a more thorough response. "He seems like such a nice boy."

"Who, Derrick?" I asked. She hadn't met him, as far as I knew.

"No, Gregory." She still wasn't really looking at me. And her words were quiet.

Part of me wanted to ask what was going on, but the other side of me didn't. It could have been a million things – work, rebuilding the house, dealing with the insurance company over our, uh, other house fire in New York...

"Yeah, he is," I said. "Which is probably why Dad let him come to my room with me, unchaperoned." I waited, but when she didn't say anything, I decided to toss out some bait. "I wonder if Dad would be cool with Mill doing that."

That got a response. She arched an eyebrow and pursed her lips. "Funny, Cassandra." She rose from the table, sighing heavily again. "I'm sorry. You haven't really ever had to deal with something so traumatic at school. You must be feeling...well, quite a bit."

"Not the worst, but," I said, "yeah, it was a rough day."

"A rough day…" Mom said, wiping her hands on her slacks. "Yeah. Well, I am going to go make some tea. Would you like some?"

"Only if it's iced," I said. "Because I think the hot tea will only be slightly cooler than the temperature outside."

Mom smirked and made her way to the kitchen. "Earl grey. Content yourself with disappointment." Her smile faded. "Life's going to be full of them."

I watched her go, shoulders slumped, moving slow and I wondered what sort of things she might be dealing with. Mom's job was tough, but usually she kinda had it on lockdown. Whatever it was, I contented myself with the knowledge that it couldn't be as bad as werewolves.

Chapter 8

"Good morning, Queen of the Paranormal," Xandra greeted me as I walked up to my locker, flashing me a wide grin. Today she wore her long, blue hair in two French braids, revealing all of the different shades of blues and a few greens that her hair had been over the last few months. It was impressive, really.

"Would you please not call me that?" I said, stifling a yawn. The school was buzzing around us with activity and some kid walked past in the opposite direction, strong coffee wafting past with them, almost making me *Exorcist* my head around to follow my nose.

"What? I think it has a sort of ring to it," Xandra said. "The sort of ring that I like and I'll keep on saying because of it."

"Any ringing you're hearing is probably just early onset tinnitus from listening to Maroon 5 too loud. Or at all, really." I rolled my eyes as I changed out books at my locker. Drop off math and history, pulled out English Lit, lightening my load by half but also making my backpack 50% less effective to swing at any werewolves or zombies that happened to invade our school today. Hey, you never know.

"Don't be a hater. So why'd you just like stop texting me last night?" she asked as we headed up the stairs toward the junior hallway.

"Oh, I totally forgot to tell you," I said and ran through a quick summation of Gregory's visit.

"So wait, he didn't know about Derrick's dad being a—"

I gave her a leveling glare. "I don't think anyone knows that, possibly including Derrick."

"Right, right, I wasn't going to say it," she said.

"Yeah, keep that word on the DL," I said. "Oh and Mill never called me."

Xandra rolled her eyes dramatically. "Mill this, Mill that. Part of me wishes you were obsessing about turning grain to flour."

"What?" I asked as we passed a troupe of drama students loudly reading a passage about being true to thine own self. "Am I talking about him too much lately?"

"You're in the lovey dovey phase. I sort of expect nothing less," Xandra said with a teasing glint in her eye.

My cheeks burned. "Well, fine. I'll shut up about him. I'm angry at him, anyway."

"What's that like?" she asked. "Does he do it like a modern boy, or like 1850's style, where he sends a sternly worded letter to your parents about your behavior? 'Dear Sir and Madam, I have occasion to scribe this letter to you today on the commencement of your daughter's ill humor regarding a jest I made on the 5th of April this year—'"

"You are in rare form today," I said, snugging my backpack tighter over my shoulder. "As far as I know, Mill does not correspond with my parents, old-school or modern, text-message style. He does kinda seem like an old school guy, though, in that I haven't heard from him since I stormed out of his place."

"You brought him into the modern age with that one, I guess." Xandra's lips pursed impishly. "He's probably just used to having his suitors – no, suitress – wait, what did they call women in his day?"

"Property, probably." I shrugged. "I don't know. I'm a little more focused on the here and now and..." My voice trailed off as my eyes fell on Derrick. He was standing alone at his locker just down the hall, pulling books from the top shelf, his face blank.

That seemed like the perfect excuse to insert myself. Gregory wanted my help and well, he would get it. Maybe not the way he imagined, but he would get it.

"Okay, I gotta jump," I said. "Have to talk to Derrick."

"Wait, what?" she said, dodging out of the path of a couple

of senior wrestlers who were guffawing about something. "You're actually going to get involved with all this now? I thought you were joking. Besides, if you're trying to ditch the 'Queen of the Paranormal' title, this is not the way."

"I guess I'll just have to outgrow it by becoming queen of everything," I said.

"This is America, we don't do royalty here." She paused, thinking about it. "Except maybe the Kardashians in a certain segment of our society and let's face it: that's a serious piece of social commentary about the state of us right there."

"Yeah, yeah," I said, waving her off. Once I was on final approach to Derrick's locker, I said, "Hey," as brightly as I could muster. "What's going on?"

Derrick turned to look down at me. His eyes were bloodshot and strained. He had bags under his glacier-colored eyes and there was dried toothpaste in the corner of his mouth like he'd picked up rabies from his dad or something.

"Oh, hey, Cassie," he said. He gave Xandra a quick glance. She waved at him, her blue hair bouncing and only a couple shades off from his eyes, I noticed. "Not much. How about you?"

I leaned against the locker beside his. "Fine. I just wanted to see how you were holding up after yesterday."

"My dad sent the entire school into lockdown." He blinked at me.

I just stared back. "I know. I was there."

"Well," he said, drawing a long breath, "I've traumatized some students, especially kids in the younger grades. A lot of them are pretty angry with me. They expressed their feelings all over my Instaphoto, my Snoopchat and I found about ten thousand notifications when I woke up and checked my phone..."

His face fell and he closed his locker door with more force than I think he intended. "So yeah...I'm great."

"Don't let it get you down," I said, catching a few freezing glares from a crop of freshmen girls as they passed. "In their heart of hearts, they know it isn't your fault. In time, they'll figure it out." Another group went by, senior girls this time and their looks were the same sort of disgust Xandra manifested the time I suggested she should let her natural hair color grow out.

"Then why are they acting like I'm the leper now or something?" Derrick still stared at his locker, even though it was now closed. "Some kid this morning told me that I should just go to a different school."

"Not cool," Xandra said, worming her way into our conversation. "But you've got friends, right? How are they treating you?"

"Most of them are totally avoiding me now," he said, not looking up. "Paul Grantham – who I thought was my best friend – told me that he couldn't hang out with someone whose dad was a psychopath killer."

"Ouch." My heart sank. Why were teenagers so mean? "What about Gregory?"

"Holt?" Derrick said. He paused to think. "You know, he's been the only one who doesn't act like I'll give him the plague."

"This is just...so wrong," I said. "You know what? *We* should totally hang out."

Okay, so I wasn't totally honest with him about *why* I wanted to hang out with him. Yeah, it was a real a-hole move for his friends to up and leave him at this, his worst possible time. Some friends they were. It made me realize how lucky I was to have Xandra in my life, who backed me up pretty much no matter what happened. More people needed a Xandra on their team.

"Um...okay?" Derrick said, looking at me questioningly. "Sure?"

"And Xandra, too," I said, grabbing her arm and pulling her against my side.

"Who, me?" Xandra gaped like a fish for a second until I elbowed her lightly on the arm. "Yes. Totally. I am in and for pitying reasons—" Another elbow shut her up.

"We are going to hang out," I said and then pointed to a group of sophomores that were glaring as they walked by. "Because we don't think you are responsible for your dad being a giant jackass and messing up one day of our young lives. Unlike some others around here."

"Well, I guess that I'm heading to the same class as you are right now." he said.

"Great, let's all go together," I said, falling into step beside him and Xandra following closely behind.

"Okay. Sure. If you want to catch a social plague..." Derrick shook his head, feigning a laugh.

It was awkward, yeah. It definitely was. But it wasn't like sending him a friend request on Instaphoto was going to do the trick.

This was good, I thought as we headed down the hallway. We were moving forward. I could almost feel the social freeze, though, the subtle chill as conversations ceased or moved to whispers as we got close. It sucked and I gave a good glare everywhere I thought it might have any impact, but protecting Derrick's feelings wasn't the point of this and I kept that in mind as we walked. There were other priorities, after all. He may have been an outcast here, but we had to protect Derrick from his crazy werewolf dad. Because as much as it sucked to be the subject of ire and distaste here in the halls of the school, it beat the hell out of being turned – or worse, eaten alive – by his father.

Chapter 9

"Well…um…thanks, guys," Derrick said. "I mean, you kind of walked with me to every class…even if you weren't in them."

"No problem at all," I said. Okay, maybe I had taken my new charge on a little strong.

Okay, a lot strong. But we gained trust. It was all in the name of gaining trust.

We were standing out in front of the school, in the blazing heat of the afternoon sun, me, Xandra and Derrick. The buses were rumbling in the distance as they started up, ready to haul kids home to their suburban neighborhoods and a horn honked over by the parent pick-up loop.

"Well…I guess I'll see you guys tomorrow," he said with a wave, turning away from us.

Now, a normal person would have been like, "Yeah, okay, see you later, new friend. I should definitely give you some space and allow you to process your day on your own!"

But not me and not when a werewolf was involved.

"Wait," I said, hurrying after him. "We'll go with you."

"We will?" Xandra said, following after me like my shadow.

"To my house?" Derrick asked, hesitating. "Because I'm going home now. You know, to do homework and stuff." By 'and stuff' I assumed he meant 'play video games'. Which I found boring.

"That's totally cool," I said. "We can just do it all together." Oof, a lie. Backsliding and I recognized it as such, puckering my lips as it escaped them.

"Really, you guys, it's okay," Derrick said. "You don't have to walk me home. I live all the way over in Westbrook. That's a long way to go in this heat."

"No big, we do it all the time," Xandra said. "Besides, it's on our way home, too."

"All right," he said, finally giving up. "I guess if you're headed that way, too…"

As we walked, I realized that Xandra and I had walked this way home together almost every day after school, just like she told Derrick. But that this was also the path we'd taken that first night that Byron walked into our lives.

It was weird to consider that because of that psychopath she and I became friends.

I glanced at Xandra, who looked back at me. Something in her eyes sparkled in knowing recognition and she nodded. She must have been thinking the same thing.

We came to a street corner and Derrick's steps slowed. Now he and Xandra were arguing something about a video game. I was walking in silence, the soles of my shoes scuffing against the rough concrete sidewalk.

"Rangers are the best, seriously." Derrick said. "They have the best chance to do critical hits."

Xandra shook her head. "No way. Mage wins. You wanna deal lots of damage? Destruction spells and staves. You want to help your teammates? Using healing spells and potions like whoa."

"Not that I'm not enjoying this argument," Derrick glanced at his watch, "but you know, guys, really, I can take it from here on my own—"

But the rest of his words were cut off as the sound of screeching tires filled the air. I looked up the street and saw an old red Dodge sports car peeling up the road toward us.

"Holy crap," Xandra said. "Slow down, buddy. Kids live in this neighborhood."

Derrick's eyes widened as the car came closer.

"Guys—" I said, grabbing them both by the arm and yanking them off the sidewalk. I was glad I did, because in that same moment, the car jumped the curb toward us, tires clanging in protest as they met pavement hard and leapt up onto the grass.

On the other side of the windshield, I saw the same face that had appeared in the window of my math classroom the day before. His eyes were wide, wild and fixed on Derrick.

It was his dad.

Chapter 10

"Is that...?" Xandra asked as the man behind the wheel threw open the driver's side door.

"How did he – ?" Derrick was almost choking on his words. "The police – they're supposed to be looking for him. How did they not—"

"Derrick." The shout was harsh, almost like a bark. His dad stepped out of the car, stalking up onto the sidewalk. Every step seemed to ring out like a gunshot.

"What are you doing here?" Derrick just stared at his father. "Why are you doing this, Dad?"

"I've already tried to tell you, but you won't listen," his father said through gritted teeth. He wasn't snarling yet, but I wouldn't be surprised if he started to. "Come with me."

The desperation in his tone just dripped. He seemed... frightened, almost, his eyes holding a sort of longing that was buffeted by rage. He licked his lips and it reminded me of a dog.

"No," Derrick said weakly, shaking his head.

"Derrick, it is very important that you come with me," his dad said, reaching out his hand. His dad stood on the stretch of grass that separated the sidewalk from the road, his car's driver-side wheels up on the curb.

We, on the other hand, were up on the lawn, only the bare sidewalk between us. A house was behind us, I saw quickly, with a fenced yard. If we tried to retreat in that direction, odds were good Derrick would faceplant into the grass while leaping the fence. Just a guess on my part, based on my observations of his coordination. That wouldn't be good for anyone, except maybe Derrick's dad.

"Why would I come with you?" Derrick spat. His voice shook and his face was dark. "Do you have any idea what you've done to me? How you've ruined my life."

"Every teenager says that," Derrick's dad said.

"I mean it," Derrick said. "You have ruined...everything. My friends won't talk to me—"

"I've seen your other friends." Derrick's dad's eyes scanned over Xandra and I quickly, then he shook his head. "You look like you've upgraded, especially in the looks department."

"What. A. Pig," Xandra said, standing shoulder to shoulder with Derrick, me on the side of him.

Derrick's dad let out a sound of frustration that sounded way too much like a snarl. "There are bigger things happening here than your little teenage school problems." He started pacing back and forth on the grass, rubbing his forehead. "It's time for you to grow up, son. To accept the responsibility that entails. Now...come with me."

"Are you crazy?" Derrick said. "Did you even hear anything I just said?"

His dad stiffened, a subtle hunch appearing at his back. I stared at it and shared a look with Xandra. It hadn't been there a moment before and to me it suggested a transformation process, or at least the possibility of one.

"Let's just turn down the temperature on this, daddy-o," I said, looking right at Mr. Bauer. "See how I subtly appealed to your inner dad, there, with the thermostat reference?"

"I caught it," Xandra said. "Subtle, but very much on point."

"Go home, girl, this doesn't concern you," Mr. Bauer said, sparing me only a quick glance.

"Dad, come on," Derrick said. "They're just my friends. Leave them out of this."

"I'll leave them out if they stay out," he said, his gaze hardening.

"I think it's best if you leave, Mr. Bauer," I said coolly to him. My hands weren't trembling. My voice was steady. I wasn't afraid. Because one werewolf had to be way easier to take on than thirty vampires, regardless of how dirty they fought.

"You." Mr. Bauer turned his full attention to me. "Who are you?"

"Derrick's friend, like he said." I stared him down. "I think that you should get gone before I call the cops on you. Again."

He let out a growl, thrashing his head around like a dog ready to pounce. His eyes never once left me and that hunch on his back grew subtly taller, his head lowering.

Derrick shuddered behind me and Xandra was still keeping her distance.

"Why is everyone trying to keep my son away from me?" Mr. Bauer's teeth showed between his lips, which were stretching at the edges like he'd swallowed a razor blade sideways. "He's *my* son. Mine!"

He crossed over the sidewalk toward us, moving quickly but not as fast as a vampire. In all the fights I'd seen with werewolves, which wasn't many, I'd seen them act as a group, trying to take down their foes from all angles. They used their numbers to their advantage, not their speed.

Even still, he had a lot of strength. He darted toward Derrick, but I slid between them, shoving Derrick with an underhanded push of my palm, sending him back as Mr. Bauer lunged for him.

Mr. Bauer snarled and tried to dart around me, but I moved to block him again, sliding like Michael Jackson doing the moonwalk.

He towered above me, his shoulders curled in, his teeth bared, his chest heaving. I caught a whiff of his breath and man did he need a milk bone or a toothbrush to take the edge off.

Darkness passed over his face once more, like a shadow and he tried to shove me out of the way.

Bad move, wolf boy.

I grabbed his arm and yanked him toward me. Just before he collided with my shoulder, I stepped out of the way and he stumbled away from us, now ungainly on two legs, as though his partial transformation made him the worst of both worlds, wolf and man.

"Dad, stop," Derrick said. "This is insane. You're fighting with a teenage girl!"

He hit the ground, landing on his palms, sending dirt and sand flying and I worried that I might have actually hurt him in some way. I didn't exactly have a weapon, but maybe a good punch to the nose would be enough to disable him. Especially if I broke it.

He was on all fours and for a second, I worried that he might try to shift right there –

He whipped his head around, staring at us and the sight of his eyes made my mouth fall open. They were dark and feral looking, nothing like the eyes of the werewolves I'd met before. Those had been clear and it was obvious they were in their right mind.

Mr. Bauer, however, had the look of a real wolf. He bared his teeth and I realized that they were now jagged and long. His jaw and nose seemed to grow more pointed with every passing second.

Oh, crap. This wasn't good. If he transformed...

He'd overwhelm us. Xandra and I would probably get hurt. Derrick would be kidnapped. And there'd be nothing I could do.

Time seemed to pause as we stood there, Mr. Bauer on all fours on the ground, little hairs elongating on his face, his eyes a dark shade, tending toward black in the afternoon sun. I could almost feel his rage, like impossibly small sparks of electricity running across my skin.

But just as quickly as Mr. Bauer's face darkened, it cleared and I wondered if I had even seen the distortion in his face, in his form, or if it was just a trick of the light.

He pushed to his feet, the hunch on his back now gone. He gave us all one last look, not saying a word, his gaze lingering lastly on Derrick, before he turned and ran back to his car. He threw himself into his front seat and the car into reverse with a thump as his tires left the curb. His engine revved as he burned past and I caught one last look at dark, angry eyes as he drove off down the street, leaving us all behind.

Chapter 11

"Did you see that?"

Understandably, Derrick was...well, freaking out.

"Did you see his eyes?" His hands were clasped on either side of his face and he had no color in his cheeks. His blue eyes were staring up the road after his dad's car, which had just disappeared from sight.

Xandra was giving me a look. None of this surprised her, though I could see that she was still concerned. A werewolf was an entirely new set of trouble, because we didn't have the protection of daylight from them. They could attack at any moment, as demonstrated by his dad's appearance.

"Something's wrong with him," Derrick said in a low voice. He was starting to pace up and down the sidewalk, fighting with himself. He seemed to be torn between fury and terror. "What is going on?"

Xandra was still giving me that look.

I shrugged. *What do you want?* I asked with my gaze.

Tell him, she mouthed.

Why me? I mouthed back. Why couldn't she tell him? Why did this always fall on my shoulders?

Derrick was facing away from us, one hand knotted in his blond hair. He was watching in the direction his father had gone, as if afraid that he was going to come roaring back around the corner at any moment.

"Hey, Derrick?" I asked as gently as I could, as I remembered why it always fell on me.

Because somehow, the recovering liar had become the one who now had to bring the truth.

"Cassie, what were you doing fighting with my dad?" he asked, wheeling on me as though the mere sound of my voice had set him off. "That was stupid. You don't know what he's capable of. He could—" he said, pausing, almost disgusted with himself for thinking about what he was about to say, "He could've hurt you, Cassie."

"Derrick, I have to tell you something about your dad," I said, drawing a deep breath.

He stopped. "I – what?"

I sighed and looked to Xandra for support. She nodded at me.

"No easy way to say this." I kicked at the tangled St. Augustine grass beneath my shoe. "Your dad…" How could I say this without sounding like a complete loon? A moment's contemplation reminded me that really, there was no way to avoid that, so might as well just say it. "Your dad…is a werewolf."

I waited for him to reply.

When he didn't, I sighed.

"…a formerly Amish werewolf," I said, continuing on. Maybe the absurdity of the statement would cause a reaction, or at least a reply.

Nope. Nothing.

"Maybe you could've left out the part about the Amish?" Xandra asked. "It's such a weirdly irrelevant detail."

"Yeah, what does being Amish have to do with it?" Derrick asked. His voice was strained and it cracked a little at the end of his question. Easy there, fella. Pretty sure you went through puberty already.

"There's a hot bed of werewolves in their community," I said, with a shrug.

Derrick was moving his lips like he was trying to form words. "W…what?" he finally croaked out.

"Trust her, she knows paranormal. She's killed vampires," Xandra said, as if she were my posse and we were in the middle of some smack-talk battle.

"Ixnay on the ampire-vays," I said to her.

"Are you speaking Pig Latin?" Derrick's eyes were wide. "Do you really think I can't understand you?"

"I thought it was a dead language."

"That would be actual Latin," Derrick said.

"Are you sure? I remember reading something about iGen not understanding – Never mind." I shook my head.

"Vampires? Seriously?" His voice was cracking again. "This isn't funny. Not at all, Cassie."

"I'm not trying to be funny," I said. "I realize this sounds ludicrous, but—"

"No, it doesn't sound that way. It *is* ludicrous!" he snapped. "Werewolves? Vampires? Did your fight with my dad knock a few screws loose?"

Well, that was a new one.

"No," I said. "Look, I get that this is hard to digest, but it's the truth, whether or not you agree with it."

"Now you sound like my dad," Derrick said, folding his arms over his chest.

"You said yourself that he looked crazy just a few minutes ago," I said, gesturing to the spot on the sidewalk where he'd been standing. The gravel was all kicked up and smeared from where he had taken off back to the car. "You mentioned his eyes. And yeah, we saw it, too."

Derrick shook his head. "This is insane. I don't even know you. Why would I believe your bizarre story about all this?"

"I'm not asking you to trust me, exactly," I said, but no, I guess I really was asking him to trust me. "I'm just telling you the truth about what's going on. These are things that you need to know."

"How could my dad be a werewolf?" Derrick asked. "I've never seen him...*transform* or anything like that."

"You said he disappears a lot, right?" I said. "Could it be, oh, I don't know...about every thirty days?"

He glared at me. Finally a, "Maybe," escaped him.

"So, like...every full moon?" I asked.

"That's ridiculous," Derrick said.

"You also told me that he'd been acting wild lately, that it had pushed you all apart. You used that word specifically. Your mom is divorcing the guy, for crying out loud."

His face turned red, but he said nothing.

"I'm not the enemy here, Derrick," I said. "And honestly, I'm probably the only one in this entire state who can help you. Because I'm pretty sure you aren't going to stumble upon someone else by accident who just happens to know about werewolves and vampires and faeries like I do."

"You know...I was just thinking the same thing," he said darkly, his hands balling into fists. With a pivot of his shoes in the dirt, Derrick started up the sidewalk away from Xandra and I.

"Wait, Derrick," I shouted after him, hurrying to catch up to him.

He held up his hand in the air. "No," he said. "I think I'm good. I'm sure you feel sorry for me because of everything I have going on, but I don't need help from a crazy person."

"But you aren't safe," I said.

Another wave of his hand, as he shoved the other into the pocket of his jeans. "And you can help how? I mean, seriously. Werewolves? Vampires? Do you even hear yourself?" He just shook his head, walking away and I did not bother to follow him.

Chapter 12

"Well, that could have gone better," Xandra said, crossing her arms.

I sighed, staring after Derrick, my heart a tangled mess in my chest. "Thanks for that helpful summation." I turned to give her the stink eye.

There was nothing we could do, save chasing after him, tying him up and dragging him along to meet Mill or Iona. Or maybe Lockwood. Any one of those three might be able to open his eyes to the truth of the improbable paranormal weirdness in our world. But then I'd probably get charged with kidnapping and how was I going to help him from juvie? Stupid non-paranormal world and its rules and laws.

"What are you smirking about?" Xandra asked as we set off across the street, toward our own houses.

"I was just thinking about the fact that no one would be able to take me if I went to prison," I said. "I know too many ways to protect myself now. I mean, if I can take down vampires, then I don't think I have much to fear from a big mama who wants to make me her girlfriend."

It was a credit to Xandra that she didn't even ask why I was thinking about jail. "Well, yeah, you'd be making shivs out of pencils or something and you'd probably meet a gremlin that lived inside the wall of your cell or something inside. Then you'd force the whole prison into a riot, where you'd somehow miraculously escape and ride off into the sunset with Mill on the back of a Pegasus." She wrinkled her nose. "Do those exist in this world?"

"I don't think so." She had become way too obsessed with my tales of Faerie.

"In all seriousness," she said as we turned the corner onto my street, both of us wilting from the summer heat and watery humidity in the air, "he took all that news about as well as I would have thought. Remember how we reacted when we saw what Byron could do."

"Yeah, I know," I said with a sigh. "It's a lot to take in. It'd be nice to be believed, though, especially given the stakes."

"Hey, I was on this vampire and weirdness train from the beginning," she said.

"I came around, though," I said. "Byron got me there, it just took a little while."

We both mutually shivered at the thought of him and not for the first time I was grateful he was dead. The rental house came into view and I sighed. This place wasn't terrible, but it wasn't...home.

"You wanna stay for dinner?" I asked. "I'm sure Mom won't mind, especially since you aren't Mill."

Xandra smirked at me. "You talk about him enough that your mom probably feels like he's there."

I gave her a jab with my elbow. "I promise not to bring up Mill...probably."

"So much for giving up lying," she said with a quick and easy grin that faded fast. "What are you going to do about Derrick?"

"I don't know," I said as we turned onto the narrow, concrete slab path that led to the front door. A car whizzed by behind us, driving way too fast. We both turned, my heart skipping a beat and I relaxed when I realized it wasn't Mr. Bauer.

"The truth has not set you free," she said. "Seriously, maybe you should've just kept lying to him, after all."

"Yeah, but trust me, that never ends well," I said.

We stopped just outside the door and I looked around.

Life here wasn't so bad. My favorite coffee shop was only a couple of blocks away. There was a large park across the street where a bunch of kids were kicking around a soccer ball, squealing at one another with delight. There was a wind in the trees that smelled strongly of the Gulf of Mexico, salty and warm and a few seagulls cawed at one another overhead.

"Well, if we can't get to Derrick," I said, looking back at Xandra. "Maybe we can figure out what's happened with his dad. Do some digging of our own."

"I like that look on your face." Xandra's eyes flashed with excitement. "It smacks of adventure."

"Adventure indeed." I smirked and nodded. "I'm thinking we should pay a visit to our old friends...the Amish."

Chapter 13

"Holy crow," Xandra said as we stood outside PDQ scarfing chicken sandwiches we'd purchased in lieu of a home-cooked meal. Waiting around for Mom to get home had resulted in little more than a distracted frown and a vague suggestion we should fend for ourselves. Which we were now doing as a sleek black Maserati slid into the parking space in front of us, headlights, that blinding white variety, glaring off our eyelids and probably visible to aliens in another galaxy.

"This is a really swanky town," I said, trying to shield my eyes and failing. My chicken was sticking in my throat. I wondered if the industrial kitchen where they turned these things out had used extra grease today or what? "I never used to see cars like this back home in New York."

"Yeah," Xandra said. "Our part of town isn't that swanky, though. I mean, my parents drive Toyotas. I rate the likelihood I ever ride in a Maserati as somewhere slightly below the chances of me..." She lowered her voice and mumbled something I didn't quite catch.

The Maserati door opened and a tall, slim shape rose out in shadow behind the blinding lights. "Now why would any sane person," a familiar voice said, "ever want to meet Adam Levine?"

"Lockwood?" I blinked through the fierce glare. The shadow stepped forward, far enough outside of the beams that I could see that, indeed, it was Lockwood who'd emerged from the Maserati.

"That car is lit, dude," Xandra said, almost hooting, Lockwood's slight against her beloved Maroon 5 apparently forgiven in the wake of this Maserati revelation.

"I think we're lit, actually," I said, rubbing my eyes. "Like a commercial building at night."

"Come on," Lockwood said, waving us forward. "We can catch up on the way."

Xandra and I ditched the rest of our chicken by unspoken agreement and got in the Maserati. "Lockwood, holy cow," I said, sliding into the passenger seat. It smelled like a brand-new car, with warm leather, car shampoo and a minty freshness from the tiny green inserts shoved into the air vents. "I'm afraid to touch anything in here." Everything was trimmed in a pretty, soft wood and shiny almost chrome-like accents surrounded all of the tech and the stick shift. "When I asked if you'd be willing to drive us down to the Amish community, I figured you'd bring...y'know, a normal car."

He grinned at me. "Only the best for you, Lady Cassandra."

"It's like a drivable spacecraft...that probably costs more than my parents' house," Xandra said, tracing her finger along one of the intricate red stitches in the dark blue leather seat beside her.

"I don't know about that..." Lockwood said.

"What happened to the Mercedes?" I asked.

His smile dimmed. "Well, after everything that happened at Draven's there were simply too many blood stains, both human and vampire, for any detailer to ever truly make that car whole again. So I decided it was time for something new. Something fresh."

"Something only a CEO, football player, or rapper would be able to afford," Xandra said. "How does a driver afford this?"

"There are ways," Lockwood said quickly. "So...Sarasota?"

"Yep." I blinked at him. "The Amish place. I mean...I sort of assumed Mill would've told you."

"I haven't spoken to him in a few days," Lockwood said. "I had needed some time away, so I—"

"Went back to Faerie?" Xandra asked, immediately leaning forward in her seat, her eyes wide. "Oh, come on, Lockwood. You have to take me next time."

"I didn't go to Faerie," he said with a hint of a smile. "I just…had some me time."

I suppressed the chuckle. "Oh? And what does that look like for you?"

Lockwood's shoulders tensed. "I—" he said. "I found a very nice spa that one of my fellow expatriates recommended. They—"

Xandra and I both dissolved into laughter as he revved the engine up. "Sorry," I said, between laughs, "it's just really hard for me to imagine the valiant Lockwood getting his fingernails buffed and his eyes covered in little cucumbers."

He gave me a quizzical look. "Cucumbers? No, not at all. It was a fae spa. They work in the practice of magical renewal."

He proceeded to enthrall us the rest of the way to Sarasota with what a faerie spa was like exactly. Apparently, it involved drinking special teas, resting suspended in nets woven from the strands of unicorn tails and phoenix feathers and bathing in a spring of water from Faerie.

"Well, this is the address," Lockwood said, pulling up alongside the sidewalk.

I peered out into the evening, the sun low in the sky. It was the right place, I thought and the same as I remembered. The whole town was as I remembered it, really – quiet, sleepy, the sort of thing you'd expect from the Amish. The little post office down the street was closed, but several of the houses had their lights in their windows, including Obadiah and Jedidiah's. I wondered if those were candles or oil lamps or what, since they couldn't have been electric.

"I haven't been down here in years," Xandra said. "I wonder if they still make that amazing peanut butter pie at that restaurant of theirs…what was it called? Yoders?" She licked her lips.

"You just had a peanut butter milkshake," I said, glancing at her empty cup in her hands.

She shrugged. "Girl can have fat dreams, can't she?"

We stepped out of the car into the warm night air. Florida had really turned on the heat in the last few weeks and I was wondering if I had enough pairs of shorts to keep me going through the summer. I hadn't worn jeans in weeks and it was still odd to me to not have to bring a sweatshirt for the evening. Even in the middle of summer, the temperatures dropped at night in New York.

Lockwood locked his car and I chuckled.

"You worried about the devilish Amish youth jacking your ride?" I asked.

Lockwood looked a little sheepish but said nothing.

I led the way up to the front door, knocked quickly on the white washed wood and stood back. Xandra and Lockwood waited on the path behind me.

The sound of a lock being opened met my ears and I turned to see Jedediah staring at me from inside the house. He was a tall, skinny teenager with a babyish face and bright blue eyes.

"Oh," he said, his face splitting in a smile. "Cassie. How are—"

The door was pulled open farther and I saw the hulking patriarch of the community, Obadiah, standing there beside him, glaring down at me.

"Ah, it's the little human, come back to ask us for a favor," Obadiah said in his gravelly voice. "I thought that we had taken care of your vampire problem for you."

"You did and I am super grateful for that," I said. "There was actually something I—"

But Obadiah's eyes had narrowed as he looked past me at Xandra and Lockwood.

A deep, guttural growl emanated from Obadiah's chest, making the little hairs on the back of my neck stand on end.

"Fae," Obadiah breathed, but it was more like a snarl. "Get him gone."

"But—" I said.

"Magic is magic, little human," Obadiah said, his lip curling. 'And we don't like his magic any more than those witches we killed."

"He isn't—" I said

"It's all right, Lady Cassandra," Lockwood said, his face calm. "I'll wait in the car." He did, not too quickly, but at a comfortable gait. That was Lockwood. Always so diplomatic.

Obadiah rolled his shoulders, allowing the tension to leave him. "Why did you bring him with you?"

"I can't drive yet and..." I threw a glance at the Maserati. "I mean, come on. Look at that car."

Obadiah glanced at Jedediah and after a moment, they both nodded. "It's a nice car," Obadiah conceded, opening the door for us. "What of your vampire friend, Iona? She was the one who had come on your behalf last time, was she not? Her Beetle is no Maserati, admittedly..."

"I don't know where she is," I said. "I am not my vampire sister's keeper, after all." Xandra smirked like I'd just told the funniest joke of all time.

Obadiah was not in the mood for jokes. Jed, on the other hand, was grinning at me like I was some cool kid who had graced him with my presence.

"So what brings you and your Fae driver to our humble doors?" Obadiah asked, folding his massive arms across the great width that was his chest. He gestured toward the back of the house. "Walk and talk, though – chickens aren't going to feed themselves."

I fell into step beside him. "Not sure if you got the news down here – or at all, really, but a certain werewolf caused a lockdown at my school yesterday."

I saw an immediate stiffening in Obadiah's shoulders and Jed, who was following behind us, was staring up at his dad with wide, round eyes when I turned to check his reaction.

"No, I hadn't heard that," Obadiah said, lifting a small basket off a hook on the side of the house and handing it to Jedediah. He was playing it real cool, papa Obadiah. This was a man who'd been around the block a few times. "How do you know he was a werewolf?" He scooped up a handful of feed from a bag on the ground and tossed it into the chicken coop.

"Well, he looked and acted like one," I said. "He stalked, he growled a lot, grew a hunch at his back the angrier he got, his eyes were wild—"

Obadiah gave an almighty grunt. "That proves nothing." He sprinkled some more feed as the chickens clucked behind us. "Did you happen to get his name?"

"Yeah, its Bauer. Didn't get a first name."

Obadiah straightened and was quiet for a few minutes. I knew that I'd struck gold. He slowly turned around to face me again.

"You knew he was one of us," Obadiah said. "How?"

"His son told me," I said. "I already had a hunch, so I asked Derrick if his dad had been Amish. Sure enough."

Obadiah rubbed his forehead. "Jed?" He glanced over at his son. "Take them on down the road to the Bauer farm."

Jed tipped his hat and then dashed into the house.

I looked over my shoulder at Xandra and her face reflected my own surprise. Derrick still had family in the area?

Obadiah looked back down at me. "I heard you cleaned out almost all the vampires in Tampa. Killed Lord Draven, even."

Was that a happy sort of tone? Or disappointed? It was hard to tell under all that booming baritone. I wondered if he'd been waiting until Jedediah was out of earshot to bring that up.

"Well, yeah, I did," I said with a shrug. "What of it?"

"Don't think you did yourself any favors," Obadiah said, wiping his hands on a handkerchief he pulled from his pocket. "Vampires don't stay gone. They're like cockroaches. They'll come back And more of them are going to come now."

A little tremor of fear washed over me as I looked up into his stern face. "Well, I'll take care of them too, then," I said.

Xandra's eyes nearly bugged out of her head at that.

Okay, maybe it was a little too cocky. But I was no shrinking violet.

Obadiah's mouth twitched at the very corner and his eyes flickered with faint...admiration?

Jedidiah reappeared at that moment, tearing out of the front door, cramming his hat back onto his head.

"Ready," he said breathlessly, coming to a halt beside Xandra.

"A piece of advice from an old dog: Be careful you don't bite off more than you can chew." Obadiah's eyes flickered and he gave us a dismissive wave, then turned back toward a herb garden in the corner of the yard, picking up a basket that Jed had abandoned, resuming the endless work he had before him.

Chapter 14

We walked back around the house to the car, which Lockwood had running for us. Not for heat, but for the air conditioning. I wondered if Lockwood appreciated air conditioning like we humans did.

Jedediah had run around the outside of the house and when Xandra and I caught up, we found him already waiting in the passenger side. I got the feeling he'd planned ahead on this one. Xandra and I slid into the backseat and I could see Jed nearly vibrating from excitement in the front. But I couldn't feel it, because the Maserati had a great suspension.

"Where to?" Lockwood asked, glancing over at Jed.

"The Bauer farm," I answered when Jed didn't realize that Lockwood was speaking to him. I guess the suspicion of magic had been passed on to him, too, in spite of his enchantment with the Maserati.

"Which is…?" Lockwood asked. If he took exception to Jed's treatment of him, he showed no sign.

"Out of Sarasota," Jed said. "East, closer to Myakka."

Lockwood obeyed and we started cruising.

Jed stayed quiet for all of five seconds, his face utterly straitlaced, a war on display as he looked sidelong at Lockwood for a second or two at a stretch until he finally asked, "Is this a V8?"

"Yes," Lockwood said. He arched a brow at Jed. "Did you know or did you guess?"

Jed's eyes grew even wider. "Well, it's a Quattroporte GTS,

isn't it?"

Lockwood nodded.

"Four hundred and fifty-four horse power?"

"How does an Amish guy know all of this?" I asked.

Jed suddenly perked up and pointed right. "Okay, turn here."

Lockwood obliged and we set off through a less populated area. We were moving farther inland. I had learned that moving inland meant less developments, less Publix stores and more trees.

"If I'm not being like, super rude, can I ask why you, the Amish, don't do the whole car thing? Or technology thing?" Xandra asked.

"Father always says that it's because cars make it too easy to be away from home," Jed said. "It sort of makes us all independent from one another. We believe so deeply in community that a lot of elders are afraid that it would damage the bonds between us all."

"Wow," Xandra said. "Maybe more of us should get rid of cars."

"My dad wouldn't mind that," I said. "He hates driving."

We were traveling along a straight, flat road, surrounded by trees. The sun was starting to set and the sky was painted with bright pinks and oranges. The clouds looked like cotton candy.

"Here we are," Jed said, pointing out of the window at a large, sprawling piece of farmland that felt so removed from everything else in Florida. It was amazing that not even ten miles from the middle of Sarasota were these beautiful open fields.

We turned down a long, dirt drive and made our way up toward the farm. There was still plenty of light and out of the windows, I saw more cows in one field than I'd seen my whole time living in Florida, all of them out grazing. I imagined it would be almost time to bring them inside. It reminded me of home in New York, where a field just like this was across the road from my high school.

Lockwood's car was being bathed in fine dirt as we drew closer to the farmhouse. There were bright lights coming from the barn and I knew that Amish would occasionally have power to keep up their barns, to protect the animals, have heaters and keep their machines clean. I didn't pretend to understand how they justified that, I just knew that it was sometimes so.

A tall, muscular man was standing just inside the door of the barn, staring out at our car as we approached. Other children were attending to scattered chores at the laundry line or heading toward the barn with milk pails in hand. All of them stopped at least for a moment to give us a look.

Lockwood killed the engine and Jed grabbed the door handle. "Just be aware…Mr. Bauer doesn't like to have visitors very much," Jed said. "Or…anyone, really."

"Should we have called first?" Xandra asked. "Oh, wait—"

I opened the door and crawled out, my nose hit with the intense smell of farm life. Tilled earth mingled with manure. Yep. Definitely felt like I was back in New York again.

"Good evening, Mr. Bauer," Jedediah said, waving as he approached. Lockwood, Xandra and I followed after him, like we were hiding in his shadow.

Bauer didn't answer. He wasn't nearly as burly as Obadiah, but I wouldn't want to meet him in a dark alley somewhere. His beard was grey and thin, hanging all the way to his chest. His nose was bent as if it had been broken once or twice and he wore a frown that looked like it was glued in place. One of his eyes was narrowed like he'd twitched hard and it stuck.

Old Man Bauer glowered at Jedediah. "What'd you bring English around for?"

Xandra's face contorted in confusion. "Who's a Brit?"

"He means us," I said under my breath.

"Got business to talk over," Jed said. He was approaching slowly, which told me something about Bauer.

Old Man Bauer turned to me, he crossed his arms over his chest, his grey eyes beady beneath his wide brimmed hat. "What do you want?"

Not the friendliest guy, was he? Funny how he'd pegged me as the leader on this, too.

"We came to ask you about your son," I said. "He came to our school yesterday and…caused an incident. His son Derrick is in my class. He said that it was time for Derrick to inherit his legacy."

Old Man Bauer ground his teeth. After a pause, he spoke in a growl. "That good for nothing boy…" He stared around at the farm around him, then shook his head. "He threw away his entire life, his entire heritage…now he thinks that he has any right to pass it off on his son?"

One of the little boys approached from behind, holding out a pair of gloves.

"Here, Grandad," the boy said. "I finished cleaning the horseshoes."

"Good lad," Old Man Bauer said. It sounded so grudging I was surprised it came out without causing him physical pain. He gave the boy a little push and sent him back along toward the farmhouse.

Old Man Bauer looked up at me again. "Everyone else in my family saw the value of our traditions. But Thomas, my only son, decided that your world was far more interesting. My heir. I have six daughters, all of whom have been faithful. But no son. No blasted son. Good for nothing, waste of effort."

"Why did he leave?" I asked. For some reason, I really thought that knowing the reason why would lead to the root of the issue with Derrick.

"Because he was a selfish, arrogant boy who had no respect for those around him," Old Man Bauer spat.

Xandra gave me a look. "And here I thought maybe it was just the prohibitions on drinking."

"I heard he's getting divorced," Old Man Bauer growled. "Serves him right. That's his comeuppance for running off with some English hussy."

"'Hussy'…?" Xandra looked like she was torn between being insulted and laughing.

"I understand that there might be some bad blood between you," I said as graciously as I could. "But do you have any idea where Thomas might be?"

"Why are you so interested in where he is?" He glared at me. Not the worst I'd ever been on the receiving end of, but not the lightest, either.

"Because I'm worried about his son, your grandson," I said. "Derrick doesn't know his dad's secret. I don't think he even realizes that his dad is as much of a danger as he is."

That made the old man shift uncomfortably.

"Look, I know you don't know me at all, but I am a friend," I said. "I've had my share of interaction with the supernatural—"

"I know who you are," Old Man Bauer said. "The vampire slayer of Tampa."

I felt my face flush. Why did that sound like praise from him? "I just…" I said. "I want to help and I'm afraid of the lengths that this man is going to go to accomplish whatever it is he wants to do. He had no qualms putting an entire school in danger to get to his son."

Old Man Bauer chewed on his lip and rubbed his fingers over his chin.

"I don't know exactly where he is," he said. "I haven't for years. But I do know that one of his oldest friends is in Clearwater and it is a friend that I know he would keep in contact with. Now…get out of here." He waved his hand at us in a motion that would have scattered the birds from his crops. "Leave me be. And don't come back, not even if you find him." His eyes set hard, the lines around the edges like scars carved into the granite of his tanned skin. "Especially if you find him." And he turned away.

He was done with us.

"Bingo," I whispered as I took his cue and walked away. Clearwater.

That was where we'd start.

Chapter 15

Darkness was starting to fall as we left the Bauer farm. We had crammed back in the Maserati and were on our way back toward Sarasota.

I tapped Jed on the shoulder, who had once again stolen the front seat. Apparently ladies had to ride in the back of the wagon. It was annoying, but whatever, he was Amish.

"How many Amish are werewolves?" I asked him.

He shrugged. "Not all of us. But we know all of our kind that are."

That didn't help me much, but he still seemed too interested in the car to really be of much help anyways.

"That whole family is kind of messed up," I said. "Grandfather is kind of a jerk, dad is crazy. How is it that Derrick ended up normal?"

"He did just walk away from us when we were trying to tell him the truth," Xandra said.

"I guess that's a good point," I said. "Still, he hasn't had a full meltdown. Yet."

"What is your plan, Lady Cassandra?" Lockwood asked, glancing at me in the rearview mirror. "What are you going to do with this information?"

"Not sure yet. Hey, isn't that your driveway, Jed?" I asked, staring out the window. Partially because well, it was true, but also because I didn't want to answer Lockwood. "Lockwood, you should turn around—"

"Hold on that," Jed said, his finger in the air. He whipped

around and grinned at me like an excited puppy. "I'm going with ya'll."

"What?" I asked, staring up at him. "Um, no. We need to get you back to your dad."

Jed shook his head. "Nah. I can call the store later, leave a message with them for him. My dad sent me to help you guys. Can't do that from home. I've got to go with you, to Tampa."

"That's…reading between the lines a lot there," I said. "I didn't hear him say anything about going to Tampa."

Jed looked at me like a wide-eyed puppy. "He told me to help you, I'm going to help you. It'll be fine. Besides, you went straight at those vampires last time I saw you. I saw it at the fairgrounds."

"Yeah and?" I asked.

"So, you are going to go right at this guy, too, aren't you?" he asked.

"Um…" I said. "Maybe?"

"I'm in for that," Jed said. "And I'm a werewolf, too, so I can help if you need an extra set of hands?"

"I think you mean paws," I said. Still, it wasn't the dumbest idea I'd ever heard. I was going in to find a werewolf, so was it really all that bad of an idea to have a werewolf tag along?

The looks that Lockwood kept shooting me in the rearview mirror told me yes, yes it was, though I wasn't sure why he felt that way. And I knew that Mill wouldn't exactly be happy when he found out I'd gone to the werewolves for help.

Oh well. I'd cross that bridge when it came. Which would hopefully be never because this whole thing was just going to turn out to be nothing anyways. It would end peacefully and soon and before it could snowball into any further craziness. Unlike all those other times lately.

Right? Right.

This was going to be fine.

Totally fine.

Or so I kept telling myself on the way back to Tampa, ignoring the Amish werewolf hitchhiker who just so happened to be sitting in the passenger seat of the Maserati.

Chapter 16

"You're sure this is the place?" Xandra asked.

We were standing in front of a house in the Tampa suburbs. The front yard was impressively and meticulously manicured, with a small palm tree in front of the windows, a large fountain beside the door and planter boxes filled with flowers. A sleek, silver BMW was parked in the driveway and as I looked down the street, I realized that nearly all the houses had higher end cars.

"This is the right address," I said, glancing at the cast iron numbers beside the large, blue front door.

"You okay?" Lockwood asked me. He was hovering – not literally – a couple feet from me, Jed a step behind him. Jed's eyes were scanning the street, like he expected Mr. Bauer to come leaping out of the perfectly-tended shrubs across the front of the house.

I nodded. "Yeah. Let's get this over with."

We stepped up to the front porch. Pretty iron lamps on either side of the door gave off warm light. There was a nice set of new, cushioned patio furniture and another potter filled with vibrant plants. The house already looked like something out of a magazine. Nothing out of place. Nothing dirty or sandy or covered in cobwebs.

It made me wonder what we were going to find inside.

Lockwood hung back with Jed and Xandra came with me to the door. I lifted the door knocker and rapped it three times.

Xandra gave me a nervous glance. Maybe she felt like Mr.

Bauer was going to spring out of the bushes, too. After our encounter this afternoon, I understood that feeling completely. The little hairs on my arm rippled as they stood up and goosebumps scattered over my skin.

A car drove by on the road behind us and a seagull cawed in the air overhead. I could hear live music from one of the restaurants on the water just a few miles away.

I heard the door lock slide open with a click and then the door was pulled open.

Derrick standing there, peering out into the night.

In the end, after some argument, we had decided not to go seek out Derrick's dad yet, even though we thought we knew where he was. I'd wanted to, but Lockwood had strongly disagreed. Xandra had suggested that maybe I was being too reckless for little reason. When Xandra and Lockwood agreed on something, I listened. So here we were.

"Um…what are you doing here?" Derrick asked, giving me a skeptical look. "It's like eight o'clock."

"What are you, eighty?" I asked. I crossed my arms over myself. I hadn't exactly expected him to be overjoyed to see us, but he was definitely more unhappy than not. "We think we figured out where your dad is."

His eyes narrowed. "What are you, Nancy Drew?"

That was better than what most people called me at this point. "I'm just resourceful."

Derrick sighed, shaking his head. I knew he probably didn't want to talk about his dad anymore, but he was going to have to learn the truth one way or another. And honestly, it was better if it came from me than possibly at the hand of his nutball father. Who knew what he might do if he went full werewolf. Would he even recognize his son? His ex-wife?

"Can, uh…can we come in?" I asked.

Derrick looked around inside and then back out at me. I could see that he was looking for every excuse not to let us inside but couldn't come up with one that was good enough.

Xandra was right. He was one of those really nice guys. He cared too much about those around him.

He stepped aside. "Yeah, okay, fine."

I walked inside with Xandra right behind me. He was about

to close the door when Jed's hand slid inside, pushing it back open. He had no trouble with that, almost bowling Derrick over.

"What the—" Derrick barely got that out before his mouth froze in place, hanging open at the sight of an Amishman in full attire, suspenders and all, standing in his entryway.

Jed looked right at Derrick and his eyes brightened like a puppy meeting a stranger. "Sup?" he asked.

I snorted. Amish kid trying to be street. Lockwood slipped inside the door that Derrick was trying to close once more.

"You brought an entourage?" Derrick gave me a leveling look. "Who are these guys?"

"He's from your dad's old ordnung." I nodded at Jed. "And he's from the land of Faerie," I said.

Lockwood's gaze whipped around to me and he stared daggers at me. Polite daggers, because this was Lockwood, but still. Daggers.

"Yeah, okay, whatever," Derrick said as he peered out to make sure that there wasn't anyone else out there to surprise him. He closed the door.

I gave Lockwood a knowing, sarcastic sort of look as Derrick walked passed me. I knew what I was doing. Lockwood just shook his head.

Yep. I told the truth again and was not believed.

Derrick's house was stunning. It was open to a large, lavish living room. On the far end of the house, there were windows that looked out over one of the many inlets from Tampa Bay that snaked their way inland. Large, overstuffed sofas that were just like ones I'd seen at Crate and Barrel filled the room, along with bookshelves lined with books, photos and other tasteful knick-knacks. Everything screamed "beachy", in shades of blue, grey, tan and white.

Derrick's mom must have really had an eye for design.

I heard high heels clacking on the polished walnut floors and the loud, sharp sound was accompanied by a high, clear voice.

"Sweetie, who was at the door?" A very pretty woman appeared from down the hall on the wall on the left with a cell phone pressed to her ear. She had long, flowing blonde hair the same color as Derrick's and brilliantly blue eyes. Her makeup must have taken her hours, because it looked as flawless as a beauty vlogger's and she wore a black, knee-length dress that made her look like she had stepped out of a magazine. A pretty floral scarf was tied loosely around her neck.

When she saw all of us standing by the door, her blue eyes widened. "Um...I'm going to have to call you back." She hung up her call and smiled hesitantly. "Hi. Who are you?"

"They're friends from school, Mom," Derrick said, staring around at us.

She turned her eyes on each of us in turn, her eyebrow arching higher with each sweep.

"I can buy that with this girl and the one with the blue hair," she said, pointing at Xandra and I. "Not sure the middle-aged guy and the Amish boy go to your school."

"I'm Cassie Howell," I said. "This is Xandra. We do go to school with Derrick. You're right about the other two, though. This is Lockwood and Jed."

Lockwood inclined his head. "Pleasure to meet you, my lady."

She seemed a little less wary of us. She licked her lips, her eyes narrowing. "I'm Corinna, Derrick's mom," she said, folding her arms over her chest. "So...what're you all doing here?"

Derrick's eyes flashed. "Nothing good."

"I thought you said these were your friends?" Her eyes narrowed as she honed in on her son.

"Cassie was being all buddy-buddy with me today, but it's only because she was trying to make me look like an idiot," Derrick said.

"I wasn't trying to make you look like an idiot—" I said.

"And then, on our way home," Derrick said, "when Dad showed up, she tried to fight him, then tried to tell me some weird stuff about Dad."

"Like what?" Corinna asked, arching her brow, looking back and forth between Derrick and I.

Derrick chuckled, shooting me an amused look. "She thinks that Dad's a werewolf."

Corinna's shoulders stiffened for a moment and she shot me

a hard lock. Her fingers twisted the silky material of her scarf. She looked over at Jed and then back at me, then let out a slow breath. "Well, yes…of course he is."

"Of course he—" Derrick said and then blanched. "Wait, what?"

Her answer surprised me and everyone else in my little posse as much as it surprised Derrick. He looked like he was going through all of the stages of grief. He was in denial, gaping at his mom. And then he looked angry and then confused. He sort of closed in on himself, staring at the floor, scratching his chin.

"I – wait. How—"

"You knew?" I asked.

Corinna shook her head. "It's one of the reasons that we're getting divorced."

"Werewolves aren't even real," Derrick said, but his voice held a thick desperation. I didn't blame him, not really. I'd been the same way about vampires. Deny it until the last possible second.

A siren blared in the distance, cutting through the awkward silence in the room.

"Come on," Corinna said. "Why don't you guys have a seat? I'll go get some water and some snacks." She sighed. "I guess we have some stuff to talk about."

"All right," I said.

"Sure," Xandra said.

"No," Derrick said sharply. "No. Mom, this is crazy. Do you even hear yourself?" He chased after her into the kitchen.

We all sat down on the cushy couches. Xandra stared at me as we heard Derrick raise his voice in the next room. It didn't sound like it was going well in there.

"That was quite a surprise," Lockwood said under his breath to me.

"Admittedly I don't know much about marriage firsthand," I said, "but as a woman, don't you think you'd notice if your husband got all growly and hirsute for three nights a month?"

"I think so," Xandra said, nodding. "I'm not down with the hair. I'd like a husband who waxes."

Jed was leaning forward, eyes slit in interest. "You want your man to wax? To wax what, his chest?"

Xandra thought about it a second. "Among other things."

Jed looked like he wanted to pursue that further and I thanked the heavens Corinna returned before he could. She was bearing a pretty wooden tray that held a swirling glass carafe filled with water, a few glasses and a plate stacked high with cookies. She set the tray down in front of us, tossing her silk scarf over her shoulder as she did. She poured us each a glass and passed them around.

"Thanks," I said as she handed it to me.

She settled herself down on the couch opposite me, her back straight and poised like a model.

Derrick shuffled back in to stand just beside the couch, glaring intermittently at us all. He didn't sit, didn't say anything, just looked around like he would have rather been anywhere but here.

Corinna looked up at him. "Oh, come on, Derrick. Sit down. This isn't like you."

"Yeah, because this is ridiculous," he said. "Should I call an ambulance or the police? Which one would get you to a psychologist quicker?"

"I understand why you don't believe it," she said. "I didn't believe it at first, either. Not for a while. Even after I saw…"

A distant look appeared in her eyes and my heart clenched.

What was she reliving in that moment?

"How did you find out about Tommy?" she asked, turning back to me, cheeks flushed.

"I have my own experience with the supernatural," I said.

Derrick was glancing back and forth between us and his mom, as if he was experiencing some sort of out of body experience. Too many people in my life had given me that look lately.

Corinna sighed, looking at Jed. "You're a werewolf, too, then?"

Jed's eyes lit up. "Yes, ma'am. For almost two years now."

"I'm sorry you all got dragged into this." Corinna patted the couch beside her again, looking up at Derrick. "Sit down. It's time you learned the truth about everything."

Derrick hesitated, but a lot of the anger had disappeared

from his face. The high spots of color in his cheeks had subsided and he was looking more like a little kid who was lost in the grocery store, trying to grapple with this werewolf thing.

She took his hand in her own and looked right at him. "I haven't told anyone this, so you'll have to forgive me if I...struggle a little."

Derrick looked down at his knees. I felt like I was intruding on something. This was something that they should work out on their own, but since I was pretty much the only one willing and able to help them, I was stuck listening.

Cassie Howell, supernatural creature counselor. I should have Dad put that on a plaque for my bedroom door.

"There was always something...different about Tommy," Corinna said. "At first, it was like a puzzle for me to figure out, the closer I would get, the better I figured I'd understand him. But he never really let me get close to him. Even when I shared everything about me, he kept me at arms-length."

She frowned and after a pause during which none of us dared speak, she went on. "I started to notice the pattern. He would take a weekend every month to go fishing and drinking with his friends. I figured it was a reasonable thing to give him an outlet. 'Give your man some space', my mother told me, 'so he won't cheat on you'."

I could see her eyes tightening and her lips pursing. Tears were probably not far off. "It took me a long time – a shamefully long time, really – to realize that every weekend he went out was on the full moon."

Derrick looked like the words she spoke had struck a physical blow to him.

She shook her head. "I know how crazy it sounds, Derrick. It sounded crazy in my head the first time I thought. Eventually, just after Derrick turned eleven, I dropped him off at my parents' house and followed my husband. I was tired of him lying to me, coming home a mess...and then I saw..." Her voice trailed off and she looked over at Derrick apologetically.

"I saw what he turned into," she said. "I caught him just as he was transforming. It was...horrible. I never would've believed it unless I saw it with my own eyes. The way his body…contorted. The howling…" She shuddered and reached up to her scarf again and pulling it away from her neck.

Four pale, jagged scars lay long lines across her breastbone. Her fingers trembling, she gently touched them.

Derrick gaped at her and at the scars. "Did Dad…was that from him…?"

She nodded solemnly.

"How?" Derrick asked. "It looks like…"

I knew what he was going to say. Like claw marks.

"He didn't bite me, thank God," she said. "But I barely escaped. Our relationship was never the same after that." She shuddered. "Once I saw him for what he was, he stopped…trying to restrain the beast around us." She pulled her scarf back in place, concealing the scars again. "Now you know my story. Why don't you tell me yours? Like why you're really here."

"Cassie knew what Dad is," Derrick said, mumbling. He looked up at me. "How?"

"I've been around the paranormal block a time or two now," I said. "What's more important than how I know is that I know where he is – sort of."

Corinna's eyes sharpened and she stared at me. "You do?"

I nodded. "Yeah. We heard he's staying with one of his friends in Clearwater."

Corinna pinched the bridge of her nose. "Don't tell me. It's Eric, isn't it?"

"Who's Eric?" Derrick asked.

Corinna ignored him. "How did you find this out?"

"We talked to Derrick's grandfather."

Derrick raised his head slowly, staring at me like I was an alien. "Um…what? I have a grandfather?" He looked to his mom. "I thought he was dead?"

"No," Corinna said. "But he is a werewolf."

"Also, kind of a jerk," Xandra said.

"Wait, the Amish are werewolves?" Derrick asked.

"The hardest working werewolves you'll ever meet," Jed said, grinning from ear to ear, sitting up straight, tugging proudly on his suspender straps.

Corinna turned her attention back to me. "You still haven't

answered my question – why are you involved in this? Why put yourself at risk for something that has nothing to do with you?"

I looked at her searching face and I sighed. "I don't know," I said. I shot Lockwood a glance out of the corner of my eye and said, "Why is there no paranormal expert in Tampa besides me? Someone who's willing to stick their neck out? I can't be the only one who has connections to vampires and faeries and werewolves." Lockwood just shrugged. I turned back to her. "Well, whatever the reason, since I'm the only one who can, I want to try and help."

Corinna sighed, shaking her head. "You're a better person than I am," she said. "After what I've seen...I can't imagine wanting to get involved with anything like it ever again. That's why I walked out on it."

I put on a smile and it froze in place. Walk away from all this paranormal nuttiness? Walk away from vampires and werewolves and fae and all the problems they seemed to bring to our world?

If only it were that easy.

Chapter 17

My heart was heavy as we got back in the Maserati and headed away from Derrick's house. The sun had long ago set and the streetlights were creating pools of bright light along the sidewalks. Lockwood was quiet in the front seat and Xandra was humming quietly beside me.

Everyone seemed to want to give me some space as we drove. I wasn't sure why, but it gave me a chance to kind of clear my head, think through everything that I'd learned.

Corinna had seen her husband change...and then he attacked her.

I was grateful that Mill had never attacked me. I had bled all over him when we were in New York and had never seen so much as a hint of the monster I knew lay beneath the surface. I'd always known I could trust him, that he was on my side.

I couldn't imagine what it would be like to have the man that I loved turn on me in an instant and then have to flee from him. I'd never be able to look at him the same way again.

It wasn't really much of a surprise to hear that she was leaving him.

And Derrick...to not only hear the truth about his dad and his relationship with his mom, but also to find out that he had a living grandparent that he never knew? It was a lot to take in and I figured that he was in for a long, sleepless night. Though it was doubtful it'd be his first, given the events of yesterday.

I wanted to text him and apologize, but I didn't have his number and doubted he'd appreciate it if I did. It would ring hollow. After all, I was part of the reason that he was hearing about these things now. If I hadn't gotten involved, he'd have still been in the dark. While I'd learned the value of not living a lie, given the hell he was living, he probably didn't feel the same – yet.

"What do you think this Eric is like?" Xandra asked. "Derrick's mom didn't seem all that...excited about him."

"I got the same vibe," I said. "We should tread carefully. Maybe hold our cards close to our chest, you know?"

Lockwood glanced at me through the rearview mirror. "Do we truly want to go chasing after him? Mr. Bauer sounds particularly...dangerous."

"Life's dangerous, Lockwood," I said. "You can cut your finger shaving your legs and get an infection that kills you."

"This is why I don't do that," Xandra said.

Jed turned around. "But you want a man who's hairless?" His eyes narrowed and his lips puckered. "Isn't that what you'd call a double standard?"

"So?" Xandra asked. "Like men haven't gotten all the double standards for most of human history." She settled her arms in front of her. "I feel like a little settling of the scales is in order. In my favor, for once."

Jed just stared at her, face all screwed up like he was trying to decide what to make of that.

"And like I told Corinna," I said, "there is no one else to help, Lockwood. If I don't step in and help, no one else is going to. Derrick and his mom are going to be at Mr. Bauer's mercy and whatever happens, it'll my fault."

Lockwood applied the brakes and brought the car to the side of the road before putting it in park. That done, he turned around to look at me. "Cassandra, it would not be your fault if something were to happen. This problem was spawned long before you entered the picture."

"Yeah." I folded my arms over my chest. "But now I *do* know and I can't turn my back. Do you know why? Because there is no one else to help. I keep expecting someone to just step up and take this from me. Someone with more experience, with better protection. 'Oh, hi, Cassie. We appreciate your help, but we got this. Go back to your teenage girl-ery.' And then I could just sit back, knowing that the whole situation was in way better hands than mine."

Lockwood's face fell. That told me everything I needed to know about the state of help in the paranormal world.

"I didn't ask for this," I said. "But I can't sleep at night knowing that there's something I could do to help and I'm not doing it."

Xandra was staring at me with wide eyes. "That's really intense. You've got guts, girl."

"Thanks, but I just happened to be in the wrong place at the wrong time," I said. "It's all worked out so far, but meeting Byron changed things forever in a lot of ways. It was like an awakening. And I can't go back to sleep knowing what's out there."

"Mmhmm," Jed said. "That's life. Can we get after this guy now? I got chores to do."

"Take us there, Lockwood," I said. This was not the time to wallow in pity. I could do that later.

Lockwood blinked at me, tilting his head to the side. "I already have."

I glanced out of the window and my mouth fell open. "But, this can't be right." I leaned over Xandra to get a better look out the window. "It's—" The words faded and I just stared.

Where a pretty beach house must've once been was an empty lot. The mailbox was still there, but the house was gone. Bits and pieces of plaster littered the ground and there was a bulldozer sitting in the middle of the lot, silent and menacing.

"How?" I asked. "This is the right place, right?"

Lockwood pointed at the mailbox. It was the right address. But...

There was no house here.

There was *nothing* here.

We were back to ground zero.

Chapter 18

"Hey." Mill's voice was soft and gentle and held no sign that he considered anything amiss between us. Which was strange considering I'd stormed out on him just yesterday and we'd had no contact since.

I was back at Mill's apartment. Night had fallen and he was awake. He was sitting next to me on the couch, giving me a wary look. He'd fixed me a hot cup of tea, which was something I probably wouldn't have chosen for myself, given how hot it was outside, but I appreciated his thoughtfulness.

"Hm?" I asked, looking into his eyes. This close, I could smell his cologne, a subtle touch of bergamot and it made me feel calm. I probably could've fallen asleep sitting up. But I didn't know if I could with his eyes on me so intently. "What? Do I have something on my face?"

"You didn't answer me." He was watching me carefully, as though I were about to detonate, which was improbable given how tired I felt. "Are we…still fighting? It's been a long time since I've dated a teenage girl. The last time I did for any substantial length of time, they were wearing those frilly collars. So, I need you to catch me up to speed so I know what I'm getting myself into. Also," he said, raising an eyebrow, "please don't wear one of those frilly collars."

I arched my own brow at him. So he had noticed. "I've been kind of busy helping a family with a crazed werewolf dad. I hadn't really thought about it in those kind of terms, but yes, I am still kind of mad at you."

He blinked at me and then sighed. "Damn. I thought maybe it had faded already."

"I'm a woman. I can multitask."

"Then these things haven't changed all that much, it seems," he said with a shrug.

"Are you still mad at me?" I asked, folding my arms over my chest. "I mean, the way I left? Because you could have called or texted."

Mill looked away.

"You are mad," I said flatly, the anger sizzling like oil on a hot pan. "Why are *you* mad?"

"I'm not mad," he said. "But I don't think that you should be hanging out with that werewolf. They're bad news."

"This again?" I rolled my eyes. "Mill, come on. He's Amish. What is he going to do, have a buggy race? Is he in the Amish version of *The Fast and the Furious* every weekend with his Clydesdales?"

"I just don't like you hanging out with werewolves," Mill said.

I glared at him.

And then it hit me like a truck slipping on black ice. I couldn't believe I hadn't seen it before. It was so clear.

"Are you…are you having some pangs of Jacob jealousy?" I asked.

"I have no idea what you're talking about," he snapped, averting his eyes. "And why are you calling me Jacob?" If it was possible, color would have appeared in his pale cheeks.

My eyes widened. "You know exactly what I'm talking about, don't you?"

He shook his head, still not meeting my eye. "No. No, I don't."

"You—" I said, trying to stifle an outburst of laughter. "Did you read the books? Or did you watch the movies?"

Mill glared at me darkly for a long second, so long that I was almost positive he was going to start shouting at me. His hands balled into fists and I leaned away.

"That is not an accurate representation of vampires, okay? It was terrible. Sparkling vampires? Are you kidding me? We don't sparkle. *We burn in the sunlight.* Who came up with sparkling?"

I couldn't help it. I lost it and started laughing. Mill didn't seem to notice. I'd opened some sort of furious rage inside of him.

"The worst part was that the series ended so badly. There was no fight at the end of the fourth book, even though the author spent the entire book building up to one. Oh, surprise, sorry. Here is a super convenient out for my characters so I don't have to kill any of them."

I had tears of mirth spilling out onto my cheeks. I'd never heard him speak with such passion about something so…ordinary. To be honest, it made me like him all that much more.

"How can you end a series like that without a big fight? And don't even get me started on the vegetarian vampire nonsense. That wouldn't do anything. In fact, it'd make the thirst worse."

"I can tell you feel strongly about this." Speaking was a challenge, it was so hard to even breathe. Now he was glaring at me, apparently spent. "You good?" I asked.

He sighed heavily, brushing away a piece of fuzz on his dark blue shirt. "I'm fine," he said, composure regained.

I shook my head. "Wow, Mill. That was really intense."

He gave me a quick look of shame. "Yeah, well…people were talking about vampires so much when the books came out that I had to...y'know, check and see what it was all about."

"Yeah. Sure. Okay," I said with a smirk. He'd read *Twilight*. Maybe even watched it. "But…I am still getting a sense that you might be jealous of Jedediah."

"No, I am not jealous of an Amish boy," he said.

"You are," I said. "You are actually jealous."

"I am not jealous," he said, his eyes narrowing.

"I don't get it," I said. "I've been tons of places with Lockwood alone, including like a week-long jaunt to Faerie, but you aren't jealous of him. Why? He's not a bad looking dude."

Mill gave me a leveling look. "He's actually a lot older than I am. And no one mistakes him for a teenager." He folded his arms across his chest. "Besides, I trust Lockwood. He's proven himself time and time again."

"So, it's because you don't know Jed that you don't like him?" I asked.

"That makes perfect sense, Cassie. You can't tell me it doesn't," he said. He shook his head. "And I was so sure that women had changed, but no…they're still into werewolves."

"I am not into werewolves," I said. "What does that even mean? If I wanted someone furry that I could pet, I'd get a dog."

Mill, apparently, hadn't heard me. "And might I remind you that you, yourself, dealt with some jealousy not too long ago?"

My cheeks flushed. "What are you talking about?"

"Remember my fake girlfriend?" Mill asked.

"Wow, really? You're going there?" I winced. "Okay, fine, I was jealous of your fake girlfriend. Are you happy?"

"Maybe," Mill said. "You know, you're touting to everyone that you've stopped lying, yet here you sit, lying through your teeth as easily as—"

My blood boiled as I stood up. "And I'm done. I came over here and talked to you because I trust you and care about your opinion and you just—"

"You're getting involved in something that doesn't concern you," he said, getting to his feet, towering over me again. Lost my height advantage. "Do you have a death wish or something?"

"No, do you think I'm stupid?" I asked. "I'm trying to help because there's no one else, Mill. No one. I know what Derrick's dad is and I don't want to have his blood on my hands."

"How?" Mill asked, his brow furrowing on his dumb, big forehead. "How in the world would any of it be your fault?"

"Because I am the only one who can help," I said. "And if you can help and don't…"

"You keep saying that," Mill said. "And how're you going to help exactly, huh? You're just a human, Cassie. Sure, you've learned to fight vampires, but does that mean that you're going to go in, guns blazing, loaded with a silver bullet and kill this guy? You aren't a murderer."

That word. Murderer. I hadn't thought of killing him…

So what did I plan to do, then?

I glared up at him. Even if he made a decent point, he was still lecturing me and treating me like a child. "So what if I can't do very much? I'm trying and that counts for something, doesn't it?"

"Not if it gets you hurt and someone else killed in the process, no," Mill said.

"I'm done," I said and I whirled around, stalking toward the door.

"Wait, you're leaving again?" he said, his tone completely changing. "Come on, Cassie—"

"No," I said, holding a hand up to stop him. "I don't like fighting with you like this." The exhaustion was permeating every word. "When you can finally discuss this with me like a normal person, I'll happily talk with you. Until then...let's just stop. For both our sakes."

Mill's eyes darkened. Part of me wanted to hurt him. I came to him for help. And all he wanted to do was harangue me for seeking werewolf help. There were people involved who could get hurt. Why couldn't he see that?

"Besides, I'm not interested in Jed," I snapped at him as I scrambled to get my keys and phone off the long, narrow table along the wall. I saw that he had fresh lilies there for me today. My heart squirmed a little, but I ignored it.

"Come on, Cassie..." he said gently. "Just stay for a little bit. Let's talk this out."

"No," I said. "I'm leaving. That's the thing that women in the 21st century do, Mill. We leave. At least, it's what some of us do."

I pulled open the door and shot a nasty glance over my shoulder at him.

"We even drive our own cars sometimes," I said. I nodded my head sharply. "Adieu."

I was getting too used to slamming his front door.

Chapter 19

I got an Uber home, texting Mom and Dad to let them know I was on my way back while I stood on the sidewalk, waiting for my ride. Because even in a world of vampires and werewolves and fae (oh my!), we still feared stranger danger. My heart was still hammering inside my head and I just kept replaying my conversation with Mill over and over in my head. It was going to take me a while to calm down.

I may have not liked Mill's stance toward the werewolves, but what he said about my endgame in this did make me think. What was I going to do? What was the goal?

Would it have to end in Derrick's dad's death? That seemed extreme, right?

But if it didn't end with that, then what would end it? Maybe the police would arrest him before things got too out of hand. That would solve things.

Except it wouldn't, because he was a werewolf that was off the rails. If he was locked up, he'd be a danger to every inmate he was incarcerated with. And it wasn't like every prisoner in the penal system was purest evil, shat out of the bowels of hell.

A car slowed down, pulling up to the curb and stopping in front of me. It was the Uber and for a second, I'd forgotten I was waiting for it. I pulled open the back door and slid into the back. I gave her my address and we started off.

I lost myself in my thoughts, brain swirling. I was like a dog chasing a car. What the hell was I going to do if I caught Mr. Bauer?

The Uber dropped me at the corner and I wandered up the street toward our rental, trying to not feel too sorry for myself. There were sprinklers spraying in a few yards, the sulfur smell of the water strong in the night air. The air was humid and the back of my shirt was sticking to my skin.

I was tired. Really tired. My limbs ached and there was a sharp pain at the base of my skull. My boyfriend and I had experienced a lovely series of fights now. Yay. Totally normal.

"I'm home," I said as I stepped inside the house. It was a relief to be back in the air conditioning. My mouth watered as I smelled a wonderful, garlic aroma from the kitchen. Dad had made something Italian and I was starving.

I wandered into the living room and found Mom and Dad sitting at the dining table. Mom was pinching the bridge of her nose, staring at the painted wooden surface of the table. Dad was rubbing her arm affectionately.

"Um, hi?" I said, snagging a roll out of the basket on the counter as I walked closer. "What's going on? Who's dead?"

Mom straightened and closed the binder that was underneath her arm with a quick snap. She looked just a little alarmed, like I'd caught her doing something improper. Which I never did. "Hi, Cassie," she said, an octave higher than normal. "How was your day?"

"Fine," I said, through a mouthful of the roll. "But again, who's dead?"

"No one," she said. There was a lot of strain in her voice. "We've just been talking."

"About?" I asked, leaning against the doorframe that separated the kitchen from the little dining room.

"Nothing," Dad said. "Don't worry about it."

"Uh, huh," I said, arching a brow at them.

"It's nothing," Mom said, moving the binder farther away from me.

I snorted. "Wow and I thought I was the biggest liar in the house. You guys need practice if you want to be believable. I could give you some pointers if you want."

Mom glared at me. Her eyes were bloodshot and I immediately regretted teasing her. Had she been crying? Or just pulling late nights?

"It's nothing that you have to worry about," Dad said a little more gently. "It's adult stuff, you know. Bills. Insurance matters. Work things."

"You're having problems with insurance bills at work?" I asked, looking at Mom.

She rolled her eyes at my adulting mash-up. "It's nothing." A little more insistently this time. That was the sort of *nothing* that always meant *something.*

"I know you had dinner with Xandra, but I left you some extra Bolognese in the foil wrapped tin in the oven," Dad said. "The pasta is in the fridge, you'll have to heat that up if you're hungry."

I could take a hint. They were trying to get rid of me. But honestly? Chalk it up to the crappy night, or stress-eating, but I was starving. Again.

Writing this whole conversation off as "None of my business," I went for the food. I had enough going on without wanting to tunnel through the stone wall they were building between me and this conversational topic.

"So, how was your day?" Mom asked, passing through the kitchen. "How's your friend?"

"You'll have to be more specific, Mom," I said, closing the fridge, the Tupperware of pasta in my hand. "I have like a gazillion friends now, you know. I'm totally on track to become second runner-up to the Spring Formal Queen." I frowned, thinking about it. "Actually, since it's Florida, it's probably all Summer Formals, regardless of what time of year they hold them."

"Derrick." She arched a brow at me. "I think that's what you said his name was?"

"Oh, right," I said. "He's doing okay. We popped in to say hi to him after we got back from Sarasota."

"Oh?" Mom raised an eyebrow. "I don't remember you asking if you could go over there."

"It's cool, we just talked about insurance and bills and job stuff." I shot her a smarmy smile as I stuck the pasta in the microwave, mashing some buttons. "He doesn't live that far from here. I met his mom, though. She seems nice, though the divorce seems to be difficult for the both of them."

"I've never seen a divorce that wasn't messy," Mom said. "I hope my firm isn't the one handling it, though. That would be a conflict of interest for me if you and Derrick are becoming friends."

"Oh, well, in that case I'll totally tell him I can't talk to him anymore," I said. "Because friendships are way less important than legal proprieties."

She snapped her briefcase shut and she smiled at me, apparently fine with my snide dig at her priorities. "You know, I think it's nice that you've taken a personal interest in helping him."

"Yeah, that's me, kindhearted Cassie," I said, sticking a fork into the bowl of steaming pasta in my hands. She probably wouldn't be happy to know that I was helping because his dad wasn't human. The relief in her voice told me that she thought I was just doing human girl things, helping her human friends with human problems.

The longer I waited to tell them, the harder it was going to be.

Even still, it sounded like she had enough to worry about right now. I squashed my guilt and smiled at her as I pulled a water bottle from the fridge. "Okay, I'm going to eat this while I finish my homework."

"Sounds good, I'll come say goodnight after my shower," she said. I caught a flash of tautness as she turned away.

I frowned. Something was really wrong to upset her this much.

I grabbed my backpack from the bench just inside the door where I'd left it when I got home with Xandra that afternoon. It was tough trying to protect people from the supernatural, especially when I still had chemistry homework to do. Juggling the water bottle, my bowl of steaming pasta that was scalding my palms and my overstuffed backpack, I wandered back through the empty kitchen. Just as I was about to turn the corner into my room, I overheard Mom whisper something to Dad in the office off the dining room.

"She would never forgive me if she knew what I was doing…even if it was for her."

I froze, my skin prickling. I listened, unmoving, unspeaking, but nothing else came. I stood there, barely balanced, until I heard Mom moving back toward the living room. I hurried up the stairs, wondering just what I'd heard.

Mom…what did you do?

Chapter 20

I think, in general, Thursday might be the worst day of the week. Sure, Mondays are bad, but at least you always know what to expect. Tuesday, a little better, you deal with. Wednesday is a day of excitement because, *yay, the week is half done, I can do this!*

But Thursday…it's like a teaser. It's *almost* the weekend, but it isn't. There's still another whole day before the weekend. But you're already done and so tired, having been through so many days of the week already. Sure, only four in actuality, but it feels like *so many*.

Tired, for me, was a bit of an understatement. I could've understood my weariness if I'd been through one of Mill's extra-long training sessions that ran and parkoured me all over Tampa. Or if I had spent the night fighting vampires, fleeing from them, staking a few as I went.

But mentally tired? That was a whole different level of torture.

I'd spent way too much time thinking about Derrick's situation with his dad before falling asleep. The things his mom had said about what she'd seen, gone through…it was haunting me. I was strangely glad that Mill was a vampire and had been since we'd gotten together. Having a boyfriend who was a good vampire seemed so much easier to cope with than a werewolf, even absent the hairiness and beastly behavior.

I stirred, sitting in my seat in class, so much of the day left to live through. The classroom was warm and it was making everyone sleepy. That didn't help. It also didn't help that our teacher, Mr. Penhallow, was rambling on about the difference between atoms and molecules. His voice was about as exciting as the hum of an industrial fan and he was spending the entire lecture with his back to us, scrawling notes so tiny across the whiteboard that I could hardly read them.

This left me with plenty more time to agonize over Derrick's situation, unfortunately.

Laura was in this class and I watched as she spent her time doodling on the corner of her notebook. Either she already knew what Mr. Penhallow was saying, or she was just as bored as the rest of us. The kid in front of me was openly snoring, a little puddle of drool staining the notebook that he was laying on.

A sharp *tap tap tap* against the window caused a stir in the class. I swiveled to look and my mouth fell open. Jedediah was standing outside the window in his Amish suspenders and hat, peering in. When he made eye contact with me, his whole face lit up and he waved. At me.

Every head in the room, apart from Mr. Penhallow, who was still rambling on, turned to stare at me.

I shrunk in my seat.

"Oh my gosh!" one girl nearest the window said. "Put the campus on lockdown!"

"They Amish don't believe in violence, moron," another student said.

"Yeah, what's he going to do, a barn raising?" another asked. He snickered with his friend beside him, who had clamped his hand over his mouth to keep from laughing.

I glanced at Laura and she was staring at me, knowingly. She'd met Jed. She knew who he was and what his presence here meant. I shrugged as the rest of the room dissolved into whispers and pointing.

Mr. Penhallow remained as oblivious as ever. How could he not notice the low din?

"Who's he?"

"Why's he looking at Cassie?"

"Why's she ignoring him?"

I looked at Jed reluctantly.

Come on, he mouthed.

How? I mouthed back, staring daggers at him. He just waved again.

I rolled my eyes, sinking back against my hard, plastic chair. This was ridiculous. This is what I got for getting involved with the Amish kid.

I raised my hand and the room went silent. "Mr. Penhallow?"

"Miss Howard," he said, turning around. "What do you need?"

Howard? Did he say everyone's name wrong? "Can I go use the little girl's potty room?"

He blinked at me, eyes widening. "Oh. Yes. Of course." He was back at the board before the classroom door shut behind me.

The school still had pretty tight security. The administrators had asked the police department to send in a few officers to protect the students, afraid that the crazy man who had infiltrated it a few days before was going to come back. There hadn't been anything on the news about him being found by the cops and I knew there likely never would be.

As soon as he went werewolf, they'd lose the trail.

There were a handful of side exits from the school that I counted on to be unwatched. It wasn't possible to get into the school through those emergency exits, but I'd be able to get out. I made my way through the halls in the oldest part of the school where the security cameras hadn't been installed yet. It was just outside of the gym and since class was in session, I was able to sneak by undetected, the sound of echoing balls ringing out through the gym doors.

I double and then triple checked down the hall, making sure no teachers or security guards were coming. When I was sure the coast was clear, I shoved my weight against the heavy metal door and stepped out into the hot sunlight.

I wandered around the side of the building, staying close to the wall and ducking under the windows until I found Jed. He was standing on the lawn, rocking back and forth on his heels, hands in the pockets of his black trousers.

"Dude," I said under my breath. "What are you doing here?"

His eyes got wide. "What?"

"Don't you understand what a campus lockdown is – never mind," I said. "What's up?"

Jed's excitable demeanor shifted and he looked around nervously. "It's Old Man Bauer. He got messed up last night, but he won't tell us what happened."

"You think it was Thomas?" I asked.

Jed nodded. "He barely let his own wife tend to him, he refused to speak about it. And that's as good as telling us what happened."

"You think Thomas attacked him?" I asked. "That seems awfully convenient, especially after we were just over there to speak to him."

Jed gave me a pointed look. "That's exactly what my father said. It's *too* much of a coincidence."

I frowned. "You don't think it could be because he's just embarrassed to tell the truth? Maybe he tripped and fell in the dark or something."

Jed shook his head like a dog shaking out his coat. "No self-respecting werewolf would ever trip over himself and claw himself."

"Wait, there are claw marks?" I asked, my heart thudding.

"What do you think I've been trying to tell you?" Jed asked. "And more than that, somebody saw the attacker leaving the scene."

"Okay?" I asked. "And?"

He looked at me blankly. "Um…and what?"

Oh, come on, *this kid*. "And did you talk to this person that saw the attacker?"

He blinked at me. "No."

"Why?" I asked.

"Because I came to get you," he said.

"What? Why didn't you just ask them what they saw?" I asked.

"Because I came to get you," Jed said again.

What a sight we must have been, standing there on the school grounds out of sight of the windows, him saying the same thing over and over and me about to experience a brain aneurysm. And at such a young age.

I sighed, rubbing my face. "How did you get here?"

"I got a ride from one of the drivers my dad always hires. He's waiting in the parking lot."

I laughed dryly. An Amish teenager had come to convince me to cut class. This was weird from end to end. "So you want me to come with you...right now?"

He nodded. "The sooner the better, obviously.

I rolled my eyes. "All right, let's go."

I couldn't believe I was doing this. I was ditching school. Why was I doing this? This was crazy.

But Derrick's dad was attacking people. I needed to be sure, because if he was, then he'd probably go after Derrick or his mom next. We had to find him so we could deal with this.

How we were going to deal with it, I wasn't sure.

Like everything else these days, I'd just have to figure that out when we got there.

Chapter 21

It was about noon when we got back to Sarasota. I was starting to learn the streets and exits. I also realized that I was starting to feel some mild affection for the area. It was so pretty and green and more spread out than Tampa was. Not to mention the proximity to the beach.

I made a mental note to drag Mom and Dad down here eventually…after all the werewolf stuff blew over.

Jed instructed the driver to go down a few streets, right down the street from a restaurant called Yoder's. Wasn't that the one that Xandra mentioned? We turned down another street and came to a stop a few miles down the road.

A few Amish ladies on their three-wheeled bikes rode by, their baskets between the two back wheels packed with paper grocery bags.

"Come on," Jed said, getting out of the car, giving the driver a wad of cash. I thanked the driver, too and crawled out after Jed, leaving him to be on his way.

The house we were standing in front of was a tiny little place and it seemed quiet. It had a red tile roof and cream siding. Children were chasing each other around out back and a woman in a blue dress and white bonnet was hanging her washing on the drying line.

"Mrs. Kauffman?" Jed asked, making his way out around the house.

Did he have no manners? Shouldn't he have knocked on the door, first?

Mrs. Kauffman, however, didn't seem all that surprised that someone just waltzed into her backyard and started talking to her.

"You're Obadiah's boy, aren't you?" she said, tossing a sheet over the line. She pulled a few pins from the pocket in her apron as the fabric flapped in the wind.

"Yes, ma'am," he said with a polite nod. "My friend and I were hoping to speak to your husband. He saw what happened with Mr. Bauer last night, right?"

Mrs. Kauffman glanced at her children, both of which were under the age of five. They were squealing with delight, chasing each other in and out of the sheets, dresses and trousers on the line. "He should be inside," she said, glancing over her shoulder.

Jed and I made our way to the screen door at the back of the house and I was very grateful, not for the first time, that I lived in a home with air conditioning. Sweat was already beading on my forehead.

All of the windows were open, letting in the heat and moisture. Gorgeous, handmade wooden furniture filled the house. A quilt was tossed over the back of the sofa, all checkered reds and greens and pinks. It smelled of furniture polish and warm bread.

"Mr. Kauffman?" Jed called.

A handsome man in his early thirties peeked his head around the corner from the next room. His eyes were a piercing green and his hair and eyebrows were as dark as coal. "Jed. Can I help you?"

"This is Cassie," Jed said. "I brought her with me to ask you some questions."

Mr. Kauffman looked back at Jed. "Are you here about Mr. Bauer? Your father's already come around."

"I assumed he would," Jed said. "But my friend here is friends with Mr. Bauer's grandson."

Mr. Kauffman's eyes widened. "Bauer has a grandson? Suppose that isn't a great surprise, but no one's heard from Thomas since he left."

"You knew him?" I asked.

Mr. Kauffman shrugged. "I knew him."

"Did my father tell you that he tried to attack his son's school?" Jed asked.

"I don't pity Mr. Bauer right now," Mr. Kauffman said, shaking his head.

"But Thomas left," I said. "Mr. Bauer isn't responsible for him, anymore."

"It doesn't work that way." Mr. Kauffman shook his head. "Parents always are invested in their children, even their children that leave the community." He sighed. "But this is not about the matter at hand. You came here to ask me about what happened last night, right?"

"Yes, please," I said.

Mr. Kauffman sighed. "I didn't see much. A car drove by in a fearsome hurry and then there was some shouting down the road a bit. When I went over there, I found Mr. Bauer on the ground, beaten and bloody."

"What do you think happened?" I asked.

He looked over at me. "He wouldn't say, but it looked like whoever was in that car did a right number on him. It's a real shame. Who would harm an innocent man like that?"

"Mr. Kauffman," I said. "You didn't by any chance get a good look at the car that drove off, did you?"

I hoped to find two things with this question. One, to confirm my suspicions that it was Thomas. Second, maybe we'd be able to find him if we knew what kind of car he drove. I knew it was a stretch. Unless he saw the license plate and remembered every number and letter…

"It was red," he said. "I remember that much. A car, not a van. But other than that, I'm afraid I can't help you."

Jed looked disappointed. If Jed had seen the car, he would have easily been able to tell us. Probably could have told us if it had a Hemi.

I pulled my phone out of my pocket and knew that I had drawn the gaze of both Jed and Mr. Kauffman. Technology, right?

I heard Jed's sharp intake of breath. "Are you going to Googer it?"

I looked up at him, eyebrow arching up to my hairline. "Googer?" He nodded. "Yeah…I'm going to Googer it," I said, smirk tugging at the corner of my lips. Oh, the irony of an Amish kid using Google as a verb. My fingers hovered over the keys for a second.

"What are you waiting for?" Jed asked.

"I'm trying to remember the name of the car I saw him in," I said.

"You don't remember?" he asked. "Well, what did it look like?"

"Well…it was red," I said, somewhat embarrassed. I knew that wasn't helpful in the least, but my knowledge of cars was about on par with Mr. Kauffman's. "It was a Dodge something. I saw the little ram symbol on the front."

"Dodge Viper?" he asked.

"Uh, no." I shook my head. "It wasn't that nice. I know those are the expensive ones."

"Maybe a Charger?" he asked.

I typed that in and scrolled through the photos. "No, this isn't right, either. It was an older car, or at least it looked older."

Jed's eyes grew wide. "Try Challenger," he said.

"My, son, you have quite the knowledge of those English cars," Mr. Kauffman said. His eyes were wide and just a little suspicious. I couldn't tell if he was impressed or disappointed.

"That's it," I said after the images loaded. "Definitely a Challenger." I showed the picture to Mr. Kauffman. "Was this the car that belonged to whoever attacked Mr. Bauer?"

"That seems right," Mr. Kauffman said, then took a subtle step away from me, like I had the devil in my phone. "I remember those headlights."

I turned my phone off and returned it to my pocket. "Thank you, Mr. Kauffman," I said. "That's a big help. Is there anything that you can tell us about the driver?"

"Didn't see him." Mr. Kauffman shook his head. "I'm sorry."

That figured. If he knew Thomas and had seen him driving, he would have recognized him. "All right," I said. "Well, I guess we at least know that."

"Is there nothing else you can tell us?" Jed asked him.

Mr. Kauffman slid his hands into his pockets. "Well, it

wasn't so late that there was nobody about. But it was late enough that there weren't any Amish around until all of the commotion started up. It happened right outside of Yoder's restaurant. Perhaps someone there saw what happened or got a better look at who was in that car."

"Thanks, Mr. Kaufman," I said, feeling a little like a hardboiled detective. "If you think of anything, please, uh..." I froze. It wasn't like I had a card, or he had a phone. "Uhm...tell Jed's dad, I guess?" I shot a look at Jed and he shrugged.

After a moment of uncomfortable silence, we both headed for the door and made our way back out of the house, heading toward the sidewalk. "Well, that wasn't a complete waste of time," I said, pulling my phone out again. "We learned that Mr. Bauer's assailant drives the same car that Thomas does. That's pretty conclusive in my view."

"Right," Jed said, peering over my shoulder at my phone. "See? Aren't you glad I came to get you?"

"I'm not really sure how to answer that," I said. "Unfortunately, we still don't know why he did it, or where he is."

"No," Jed shrugged. "but someone at the restaurant might be able to help us."

"Great," I said. "We're back to relying on the kindness – and memory – of strangers. Who don't care about cars. Or technology." I ordered an Uber. I felt lazy, knowing the restaurant was only a few minutes away, but it was hot and I didn't want to be a disgusting, sweaty mess on the walk over.

"Hey, it could be worse," Jed said, eyes flashing with a wicked sort of look, slipping into a slow grin. "You could be looking to rely on the kindness of English city folk." He arched his eyebrows like he'd just told the funniest joke in the history of the world.

"You have got to get out more," I said, shaking my head. Why did the Amish call everything American 'English'? The little countdown timer said my ride was still ten minutes away. I wondered if I'd melt by then, or just lose my mind.

Chapter 22

The Uber driver was a skinny woman in her forties with a bad blonde dye job and her dark roots showing through. Her muddy brown eyes were encircled by cheap eyeliner and purple eyeshadow. I had a feeling she was the type who drank nothing but cheap vodka and smoked cigarettes in her spare time. She had a nose piercing that didn't help her look any younger at all.

"I've never been in a car that smelled like fried fish before," Jed said after we'd been in the car a few seconds. She didn't have the AC on for some reason and as I looked around the small vehicle, I wondered if it was because she enjoyed the heat or because she didn't want to increase her carbon footprint by running it.

I held my breath, feeling a little pained, as the driver gave him a nasty look in the mirror. I gave her one right back. Get your car cleaned and start running the AC if you don't want a naïve Amish boy to comment on the smell.

"So, what, like, are you two together or something? Thought that was forbidden, or whatever," the driver said after giving us some choice glare for a few seconds.

"Definitely not," Jed said.

"Please tell my boyfriend that," I said, folding my arms across my chest. Little drops of sweat were cascading down my sides and back. I felt like I was soaking through my shirt.

Jed looked at me in surprise. "Oh, you mean the v—"

I kicked his foot. Idiot. He'd been about to say *vampire*. In

101

front of our Uber driver.

"…Mill?" Jed asked, blushing a little. Apparently he'd forgotten our present company.

"Yes, him," I said. I looked away from him, suddenly aware of the fact that I was in the exact same situation that Mill didn't want me to be in. Cavorting with werewolves. And I felt a little spike of guilt, in spite of the fact that I'd done nothing wrong.

"Why do you say it like that?" Jed asked. "Are you mad at him?" A little grin broke across his lips. "Are you two in a fight?"

"Yes," I said. "No," I said, just as fast. "I don't know. Maybe a little, on and off for, like, the last week or something. He's been a little sensitive because of…" How could I say it without sounding like a complete moron, but also not giving too much information to little miss nosey in the front? "He's jealous," I said finally. "Of you."

Jed blinked at me. "Wait, he's jealous of *me*?"

The driver snorted as she waited at the stop light at the end of the road. "Wait, your boyfriend is jealous of string bean here?" She shook her head. "Figures. Men are always trying to find things to fight about. Don't you let him tie you down, honey."

She looked like she had more to say and I doubted any of it was going to be of any immediate use, so I chose to ignore her. "I think he's jealous of the time we've been spending together trying to help Derrick," I said to Jed. "He doesn't really approve of…you know…your family's background—"

"Oh, so he's a bigot, too?" the driver said, swerving to avoid a pothole.

I groaned. She sounded so snotty, I wanted to strangle her.

"Honey, you need to drop him like he's hot," she said, snapping her fingers. "Any man who's as controlling as that is bad news. You need someone who can give you positive vibes and—"

Jed nodded at me, apparently oblivious to the driver's ranting in the front seat. "I can understand that. We don't care much for his kind, either. But does he think that I'm interested in courting you?"

I nodded. The driver was still going on about Mill. I heard

the words "tolerance" and "acceptance" thrown in there. I mentally boxed her out of the conversation and she didn't seem to realize it.

"I think he's a little jealous he can't be out helping me with all this stuff during the day," I said. "Plus, he just said that all…people…like you are dangerous."

"He really is a bigot," said the driver in the front. "'Dangerous'? Do we need to report this to the police, honey?"

"Shouldn't you stay in your lane?" I shot her a nasty look. "Literally, I mean. You're swerving all over the place."

She corrected and shot me a face-melting look in the rearview, which I promptly ignored.

"Well, he doesn't have anything to worry about from me," Jed said, tugging proudly on his suspenders. "I have no interest in you at all. You dress too provocatively for my taste, English. And my father would disown me if we became entangled in any inappropriate way."

I looked down at myself. I was wearing shorts and a T-shirt. Provocative? I was also sweating like a pig at this point, which maybe made the clothes cling a little, but it was hardly the stuff of a glamor mag or a *Sports Illustrated* photo shoot. Hell, I wasn't even a good candidate for the page 64 throwaway picture in a teen magazine.

"Even a hair bonnet wouldn't be able to contain all that, woman," he said to me, pointing to…all of me, as if in answer to the question I was asking myself.

I snorted. "Funny."

"Excuse me?" our driver said, wheeling around in her seat.

"Just pull over, please," I said, as she started to drift into the other lane again and I finally lost patience. I could see the diner ahead anyway and suddenly the desire for safety outweighed the need to be dry. Because I wasn't, anyway, at this point and wouldn't be, ever, in this car. "I'll leave you a good review if you just pull over now."

She was fuming, muttering about the disgusting pigs that men were and Jed was looking at her like she was some sort of alien. The tires bumped against the curb as she pulled over and I raced to get out before she could throw any more choice words his way. The squeal of her tires was over quickly, unlike the smell, which lingered after we'd gotten out of the car. The driver gave Jed the finger as she pulled away, a gesture that left him speechless.

"What kind of bee was in her bonnet?" he asked.

"Who knows?" I shook my head, watching her go. I was allowed one lie once in a while, right? Because after that ride, I had no intention of giving her a good review.

Chapter 23

"In hindsight, maybe ordering an Uber this far out wasn't such a great idea after all," I said as we walked the last hundred or so yards to Yoder's.

"It's all right, Cassie, you couldn't have known that the person they'd send to pick us up would be like that." He snickered. "I could have done better."

"Yeah, but it's not like you know how to drive."

He grinned. "Well, don't tell my father, but a year or so back, one of the English that drives for my cousin's family tried to give me driving lessons. We nearly scared the cattle to death. Father would've skinned me alive if he found out."

I laughed. "I would imagine that's a big no-no for you Amish. Driving, I mean."

He nodded and we fell into silence. The restaurant was just across the crosswalk and I could hear the hum of its air conditioning now. It gave me a little pang of joy across the skin. My shirt was clinging to me like I was its own cloth-y lifeboat in a sea of certain moisture. And death, maybe, because it was hanging on for dear life.

"I don't see how you guys stand it," I said. "Not having AC."

Jed grinned. "You get used to the heat. It's the worst in August and September. A lot of us start using generators for fans and wall air conditioning units. It's just too hot otherwise."

"Isn't that a violation of your...uhh...religious laws or something?"

If he had an answer, he didn't share it, instead falling into silence as we stepped in the front door of the restaurant. Immediately we were bathed in cool air and the smell of peanut butter pie baking. "Oh my gosh, that smells *so good*," I said.

There was a pretty waitress behind the counter, her dirty blonde hair in a high ponytail, some dark purple streaks in the underside of her hair. She was super tan and fit, maybe a runner or biker in her spare time. She grinned at us and the lone tattoo on the inside of her wrist and her lack of a head scarf answered my internal question about whether or not it would only be Amish people who worked here at the restaurant.

"You're smelling the pie, right?" she asked with a smile as we approached the counter. "It's our best seller. Table for two?" She pulled some menus from below the cash register.

"Uh, no, thanks," I said. "At least not yet. Though I might have one of those peanut butter pies to go."

Jed gave me an amused look.

"We had a couple of questions for you," I said. "Maybe you could help us?"

"Sure, what's up?" she asked, the menus falling back down like the flag in a drag race.

"Is there anyone here that was working last night?" I asked.

"Let me check," she asked, then disappeared back into the kitchen.

The restaurant was super busy for lunchtime, a pleasant hum over the classic Americana diner decor. It seemed like the sort of place that was always busy. Almost every table was filled and all of the food looked amazing and like it came out of a grandmother's kitchen.

"Do you guys eat here?" I asked Jed.

He shrugged. "Sometimes, especially if we're having a meal with some family from out of town."

"You guys live here all year round, right?"

"Not all Amish here do, but for us this is home, yes." He nodded.

The girl with the purple streaks in her hair returned. A dark haired, dark eyed girl following closely behind, her gaze glued to us from the minute she walked out of the kitchen. She was a couple of years older than me, with tanned, olive skin. Her thick hair was tied up in a bun at the back of her head and she had a little bit of makeup on, including some dark red lipstick.

"This is Blanca," said the girl with the purple-blonde hair. "She was here last night."

"Awesome," I said. "Do you mind if we ask you a couple of questions?"

"Sure." Blanca gave me a wary look, but she followed us away from the counter back toward the door, so we were out of earshot.

"I was wondering if you maybe saw the mugging that happened outside the restaurant last night," I said in a low voice.

"Ohhh." Blanca's eyes got wide. "Yeah, I did. Are you guys with the cops or something?" She gave Jed a skeptical look.

"Um, no," I said. I wasn't a cop. I wasn't a PI. I was a high schooler. I had no weight behind me at all, I realized, not for the first time. "It was the grandfather of a friend of mine who was attacked last night," I said as earnestly as I could. Still close to the truth was tough here, but necessary. "I just wanted to get some details so I can help the family out."

"That's awfully sweet of you," Blanca said.

"I figured it was best to handle it in the way that the Amish handle it," I said with a small shrug, glancing over at Jed. He nodded in agreement.

Well, maybe not exactly. Because this branch of the Amish might handle these sorts of problems by eating their enemies.

"It's complicated," I said. "I don't want to bore you with the details. The family is just trying to find anything they can about the guy who attacked him, you know?"

Blanca looked a little nervous but loosened up after a second. The friend pity story always worked. "All right, yeah. What do you want to know?"

"I know it's probably a long shot, but did you see a red Dodge Challenger go by last night?" I almost held my breath in hope.

Blanca's brow furrowed and she groaned. "Yeah, I did. It pulled in here, actually."

I looked over at Jed. He seemed to be standing up a little straighter and was I imagining it or had his ears lengthened like a dog's. I felt like beneath his pants, he was sprouting a tail just to wag at this piece of news. "Did you see who was in that car?" he asked.

"Two men," she said. "They came in here looking for something to eat."

"Really?" I asked. "What did they look like?"

She tapped her chin, shifting her weight between her feet. "Well, one guy was really tall and kind of gangly, like super thin. He had short brown hair and a close-trimmed beard and he was wearing a bright green T-shirt, like neon, blinding, ouch, offends my eyes kind of color. The guy with him was a lot bigger, like muscle wise. He had hair that was kind of wild, salt and pepper. He had this kind of...weird look in his eyes. I was worried he was drunk or something. Angular face, pointed chin," she sort of traced an outline of her own face with the tip of her finger.

Jed stiffened beside me and I looked over at him. Boom. Finally. That second description was definitely Thomas Bauer.

"So, what happened when they came in?" I asked.

Blanca's face soured. "I don't really know. There was something off about them, you know? Like weird vibes, big time. The funny guy was wearing sunglasses most of the time, maybe to hide his funky eyes." She shook her head. "I don't know, maybe he just had them checked or something."

Good explanation, I thought, but it was more likely that Thomas didn't want anyone in his old community to recognize him on accident.

"Anyway, they came in and I seated them. They seemed pretty down, so I did my thing as the nice waitress by trying to cheer them up a little, you know? It took a few tries, but eventually, they actually started talking to me."

My heart skipped a beat. Good, good. Maybe we were finally getting somewhere.

"The guy with short hair was really nice, a lot nicer than his friend. Once I made it past that shade of neon green I realized he was wearing a T-shirt for an event for a CNA company. And I was like, 'Wow, you're a CNA? That's so crazy, I'm going to school to be a CNA.'" She looked right at me. "Isn't that crazy?"

"That is...an interesting coincidence," I said, not sure what kind of a response she was looking for there. It must have been all right because she kept going.

"So he started talking to me about it," Blanca said getting pensive. "He said he's been in nursing for about twenty years now."

Bingo. "Oh?" I asked.

She nodded her head excitedly. "Safety Harbor Medical Care in Clearwater. Been around for almost fifty years. When I commented on that, he said it was his dad's company."

"Did his friend say anything?" Jed asked. Was his butt wagging?

Blanca's eyes narrowed. "Not really. He sort of nodded his head a few times. I think that he was just hungry, to be honest. Or maybe stoned. Either way, not much of a talker."

"I see." I grinned at her. "Well, thank you, Blanca. We really appreciate your help."

"Hey," she asked. "Is the guy who was attacked okay?"

I nodded. "He's fine. Stubborn enough to not talk about it."

"Oh, good." She looked over her shoulder as a group of six or seven people stepped into the restaurant. "I'm sorry to do this to you, but I really need to get back to work."

I thanked her and Jed and I stepped back outside into the scorching sun. Sweat already started to preemptively roll down my back, as though my skin could sense in advance that I was heading back into the oven that was Florida.

"So...his friend lives in Clearwater," Jed said, lifting his hat to mop his brow with his sleeve. "Safety Harbor, more specifically."

"We have something to go on again," I said, nodding. "I find it interesting that his friend is a CNA."

"What does that stand for?" Jed asked. "I was lost for that whole part of the conversation."

"Certified Nursing Assistant," I said.

Jed's eyes turned to thin slits as he pondered that. "So...like a nurse's secretary?"

"I don't really know," I said. "I'm not sure my dad works

with CNAs. I've heard him talk about LPNs. I asked him about them one time and he laughed and said it stands for 'Low Paid Nurse', but I'm not sure what a CNA does. Maybe assists a nurse." It was my turn to ponder. "Would that be a beneficial thing for a werewolf? To have a friend who has medical training?"

"Oh, yeah. Especially when he isn't part of the pack anymore," Jed said.

I pulled out my phone again and I caught a strange look from him. "What?"

"Are you going to summon another car for us?" he asked.

I snickered at the word *summon*. "Yeah," I said. "And hopefully this time I'll conjure up a nicer, less judgmental, more sane driver."

"Wow." His eyes grew wide. "Technology is really like magic. Maybe that's why all the Elders hate it so much."

Chapter 24

Safety Harbor Medical Care was located in an ugly, mustard yellow building straight out of the seventies with a wide, overhanging flat roof. The walls were barren and it was about as inviting as a prison. It was a little less well-guarded, though, fortunately.

"This is a hospital?" Jed asked. "Why is it so small?"

"It's not a hospital," I said. "It's an...office building? Clinic?" I honestly wasn't sure. It looked like it might have been trying to be both, with a dash of medical supply store thrown in for good measure. I rolled my eyes. "Doesn't matter. Come on, let's just go inside."

The door made a *ding* sound when we stepped through, which made Jed nearly jump out of his skin. He whipped his head all around, trying to find the source of the otherworldly sound. "What the devil was that?"

"Just the doorbell, don't get your tail in a twist," I said.

The waiting room was small, with two rows of metal framed chairs that looked about as comfortable as sitting on rocks. There was a small desk behind a sliding glass window, which opened at the sound of the bell.

"Hi, go ahead and have a seat," said the woman with the round face and thick glasses. "I'll be with you in a minute."

"Thanks," I said and sat down on one of the faded faux leather seats. This had the feel of a doctor's office and made me wonder what the hell they did here. The whole room smelled like bleach and cheap rose candles. The table beside me was filled with magazines that looked like they were new last year and the small flat screen television had the local news station on.

"…gave up the chase after a short time, surrendering to the police. Police sources confirm there was an undisclosed quantity of heroin in the trunk. This is the latest in a series of confiscated opioids—"

Jed's eyes were fixated on the screen, wide and glassy. He was mesmerized.

I wished that the waitress had gotten the name of Thomas's friend. That would make it easier for me to ask for him when we got to the window. Instead I was going to have to do...well, something else.

I sighed heavily, my foot wiggling with impatience. This was not the way that I wanted to spend my Thursday. I mean, school wouldn't have been any more entertaining, but at least I wouldn't be chasing a werewolf all over the central western part of Florida.

The woman at the desk slid open her little window and I jumped back up to my feet.

"Sorry about that," the woman said with a wide grin. "What can I help you with?"

I whacked Jed in the arm.

He winced. "Hey, what was that for?"

I headed toward the front desk, Jed grumbling as he followed after me.

"Hi," I said, putting on my best good-girl grin. The one I'd save for Mom when I really, *really* wanted something. The one that she was immune to now, but still worked on Dad. "I'm looking for someone who worked here."

"Name?" she asked, turning the computer sitting in the corner of her desk. She poised her hands over the keyboard, ready to type.

"Theirs." I put the grin on again. "I…don't actually know his name, exactly. His dad is the owner, though."

"We have to ask him some questions," Jed said, very seriously, with a nod of his head.

The woman gave him a skeptical look, then went to me. She didn't say anything, but I took her intense gaze to mean something like *Amish? What?*

The woman looked from me to Jed. "You must mean Eric Nelson."

"That's it," I said, snapping my fingers. "Is he here?"

"If he's not on his lunch break," she said, getting to her feet. She crossed to the back of the little office to the door and stuck her head out into the hall.

"Eric?" she called. "There are some people here to see you."

"Honestly, I'm surprised she just gave us that information," I said under my breath to Jed.

His brow furrowed. "Why? You were so polite when you asked."

"I'm a complete stranger," I said. "For all she knows, I could be a murderer. Or maybe a jealous ex-girlfriend, out for revenge."

Jed looked confused. "But you aren't."

I rolled my eyes. "No, I'm not. But she doesn't know—"

She took her seat back at her desk, smiling up at us. "He's coming."

Sure enough, a man with a short beard and short, dark hair strode into the office, looking down at the tablet in his hands. He was tall, just like the waitress said, with long, gangly legs.

"It's him," Jed said, shaking my arm. "Hey, you! Stop right there!"

He glanced up from the tablet and when his eyes fell on Jed and I, he froze. His face drained of all color and he dashed back into the hall and out of sight.

"Eric!" the woman at the desk shouted after him. "What the...?"

Jed took off after him, pushing through the doors from the waiting room and into the long hallway.

I just watched for another second, my reflexes not exactly dog-like in their speed, not for something like this. Which wasn't exactly how I imagined all of this ending up.

Still, running was the international sign of guilt. Even the Amish kid seemed to recognize that. I spurred myself into motion, hurrying after Jed and down the hall after the fleeing Eric.

Chapter 25

I nearly collided with a nurse in scrubs as I pounded down the hall at top speed. She leapt out of the way just in time, letting out a string of curses as she almost dropped the chart she was carrying.

"Sorry," I said over my shoulder as I ran. "It's a werewolf thing." I blinked as I realized what I'd just said. "I mean...it's a...you know what? Never mind." There was no way I was going to explain away the werewolf comment. Not on a flat-out run after an Amish man through a medical clinic.

I rounded the corner where a nervous looking doctor was pressed up against the wall, staring horrified down the hall after Jed's retreating, suspended back. The emergency exit ahead was just swinging shut. Now that I was on a straightaway, I picked up speed.

The thing about knowing supernatural people is that they were always faster than me. Especially since I didn't do track in high school. Or soccer. Or tennis. Or any sport that involved running in shape or form.

Or sports at all. Period. Or cardio.

Spending my time running from vampires had toned me a little and then adding the training with my vampire boyfriend and I'd actually started to build up some stamina. Not nearly enough, I reflected as I huffed, bursting out of the exit into the burning daylight. Paranormal creatures would always be faster than me and probably in better shape thanks to their natural gifts. Well, that and my hatred of running.

The bright sunshine made me squint my eyes in pain as I stumbled onto a grassy patch of dirt between the clinic and the building beside it. The humidity was just oppressive, like an over-aggressive cologne wearer. I whirled around in time to see the last bit of Jed's transformation into a full-blown werewolf. His limbs extended and bent backward the wrong way, his snout getting long and fur sprouting from his skin like a chia pet.

I did a double take, because he was still wearing all his clothes. The pants around his narrow, elongated waist were hiked halfway up his back, the bottom cuffs at his knees. The shirt was still neatly buttoned, though it was clinging tightly.

It was a wolf in Amish clothing. I stared for a second longer than I needed to, really, or maybe not long enough. The suspenders had trapped his clothes in place and he bounded off, leaving his hat and shoes just outside the door. I debated grabbing them for a half second, then passed on it. Stooping to pick them up would just slow me down when I was already behind. So I just took off after the two of them.

Jed bounded after Eric, who had taken off down a side street into a housing development. I could see them as I rounded the clinic's corner, the wolf pursuing a man in blue scrubs. There weren't a lot of cars around, which I was suddenly grateful for. What would people think, seeing a giant wolf wearing Amish clothing chasing after a dude in scrubs? I'd have to do a double take and there was zero chance I'd ever mention it to anyone I knew for fear they'd think I'd relapsed on the lying.

Eric turned down another side street, running across the crosswalk. Jed close behind him. A growl escaped the werewolf and Eric tossed a fearful look back at him.

The houses in the development were big, right on top of each other and seemingly empty. Most of the residents must have been at work, which was good for us. Less people to see us chasing after Eric, less of a reason to call the police out of fear.

Eric skirted around a large, blue recycling bin and swung out his arms as he passed it, knocking it over into Jed's path.

Jed leapt, clearing the bin easily, with a rumbling bark that sounded like a cocky laugh, something only a few degrees off what the human version of him might have done in a similar situation.

Making a sharp turn, Eric darted off between two houses. When I turned the corner, I saw Jed dive between some trees in the small forest that started behind the houses.

I groaned, trying to keep up. My chest now hurt with every breath I drew and my legs were begging me to stop, screaming in pain. The muscles in my back and side were seizing and I was sweating like a beast. Though that was nothing new. I kept an eye on Jed through the trees, his white shirt stark against the yellow-green of the forest.

I had to slow my frantic pace, not wanting to catch the tip of my toes on any roots that were snaking out of the ground. The last thing I needed was to break my ankle or something. Jed, however, was dodging and weaving around the trees like a pro. He caught Eric coming around a tree, burying his teeth in the man's ankle. Eric let out a cry as Jed ripped him off his feet and tossed him to the ground, baring his fangs.

I stumbled to a stop, my hands on my knees, panting, sweating, gasping for breath. "Wait…" I managed to say. "Jed."

Jed had flipped him over with his nose and was standing over him, paws pinning him to the ground. His teeth were bared and there was a deep, low rumbling growl. Eric, for his part, was wide-eyed and staring straight up into Jed's face.

I knelt next to them, gave Jed a pat and heard his growl lighten a little. I gave him a sideways look; he really did sound like a big puppy, especially since I'd apparently petted him.

"Who…who are you?" Eric asked, looking back and forth between us.

"We were going to ask you the same thing," I said, still pulling in deep gulps of air. "Now. What do you know about Thomas Bauer?"

Chapter 26

I couldn't imagine what it must have been like for Eric, lying there prostrate on the ground beneath an enormous, hulking beast. Jed's nose wasn't far from Eric's and he was growling low and deep in his chest, his lip curling.

I also hoped, for Eric's sake, that Jed remembered to brush his teeth that morning.

He was squirming beneath those big paws, eyes squinted shut. Eric turned his head back and forth, dragging his hair against the ground, trying to put every centimeter possible between himself and Jed's fangs.

"What's the matter, Mr. Nelson?" I asked, leaning on Jed's back with my elbow, half to look completely at ease, half because my legs were jelly from the run and I needed to sit down. "I thought you were used to running with wolves."

"I—" His eyes were wide, staring up into Jed's. "I don't know what you're talking about."

"Oh, please," I said. I stroked Jed's back, which caused him to growl even more, though lower. "I know a liar when I see one. So don't even try it." I smirked. "Besides, if you weren't familiar with werewolves, you'd be freaking out a lot more about my friend, here."

Jed gave a satisfying snarl in agreement.

Eric gasped for breath, looking around wildly.

"We know that you've been helping Thomas Bauer," I said. "We need to know where he is right now."

I watched Eric's face contort as I looked over Jed's wolfish shoulder. I touched Jed's back again and another growl rumbled out.

"Okay," Eric said, barely keeping it together. "Okay. Whatever you want."

"How do you know Thomas?" I asked. "Let's start there."

"Can — can the wolf back off a little?" he asked looking at me, but having a hard time keeping his eyes off Jed.

The fur on Jed's back stood up straight and he snapped at the air near Eric's nose, causing Eric to twitch.

"Do you think I'm stupid?" I asked. "I'm not chasing you again. The wolf stays. Right, Jed?" He barked and I patted his back again. "That's right. Who's a good boy?"

Jed looked at me sideways and made a low whimper, quietly, as if to say, *Stop embarrassing me in front of him!* I backed off the patting a little and we both looked back down at Eric, who seemed oblivious to our interplay.

"Look, it's not like I'm loyal to Thomas or anything," Eric said. "He's — he's crazy, man. I felt kinda sorry for him at first, with his wife leaving him and losing his kid. But now? He's totally lost his mind."

"Interesting," I said. "Go on."

Half of Eric's face was pressed into the sandy dirt beneath him as he tried to gaze up at me, cheek rubbing against the sand, wolf saliva dripping down in the occasional dribs and drabs off Jed's open lips. I couldn't imagine he was very comfortable.

Good. That was what he got for trying to run away from me and making me do cardio.

"Thomas and I have been friends since he left the ordnung," Eric said. "We went to college together. We kind of drifted apart a little when we got older, but we'd get together whenever we got the chance. Memorial Day, Fourth of July, stuff like that." He shifted, wincing in pain. "Seriously, if you could just get the wolf off of me—"

I looked right at Jed. "I'm not buying it. You?" Jed barked and shook his head, his comically exaggerated snout waving in a very un-doglike manner. "Deal with your discomfort by talking faster," I said.

"Okay, fine," Eric said as another drop of wolf drool caught him just above the eye. "Ew. He came to me a few years ago and told me his secret. I didn't believe him at first, but he showed me some wounds he'd gotten after disappearing for a weekend. Needless to say, he found ways to convince me and so I agreed to help take care of him. He was my friend, you know? And it wasn't like he could go to a hospital or anything. They'd ask too many questions he wouldn't be able to answer without exposing himself."

"Been there, done that," I said flatly.

He gave me a quizzical look.

"I hang out with vampires. Also fight them. And kill them," I said.

"V – vampires?" Eric said, sputtering. "What?"

"Focus, Mr. Nelson," I said, snapping my fingers.

Eric's brow furrowed, but he swallowed his questions. "Anyway, I started taking care of him when he was in trouble. It used to only be about once a month. The full moon, you know. The rest of the time, he was fine. Didn't even transform if he didn't have to. Mind you, I don't really know what he did most of the time. I assumed he was home, being a good dog or whatever—"

Jed snarled.

Eric winced. "Sorry! No offense."

I gave Jed a pat on the back. His hackles came down a little.

"But last week…" Eric said, "Last week he came to my house in the middle of the night. He was a bloody mess and he was…murderous. He said he tried to go and see Corinna – that's his wife—"

"We know the family," I said. "Just go on."

"He tried to go see her and their son and she called the cops on him. She told him she was going to get a restraining order. Well, he didn't like that. He was pissed because it was starting to look like Corinna was probably going to get full custody. It didn't really help that he was a flake, couldn't hold a job to save his life. She's always been the bread winner."

This matched almost exactly with what Derrick told me, which was a relief. It meant that so far, Eric had decided to tell us the truth.

"What happened last night?" I asked. "We know you were

with him."

Eric paled. "Y – Yeah, okay, I was with him. And he—" He swallowed nervously. "I don't know, man. He looked like my friend, but he was all beast."

Jed's paw scraped at the ground beside Eric's head. I knew that Jed and the rest of the Amish werewolves had strong feelings about werewolves who were not part of the pack any longer. Thomas had thrown away his lifelong beliefs, turned his back on his family, gone rogue.

"Why do you keep agreeing to help him if he scares you so much?" I asked.

Eric averted his eyes. "I – well, you see—" He looked up at me. "A guy's gotta feed his family, you know? And my dad's been cutting my hours at the clinic. I figured if he was willing to pay me for my services, then—"

"So you were taking a bribe," I said, rolling my eyes.

"It's not like that," Eric said. "I gotta make ends meet."

"You're playing veterinarian and chauffeur to a dangerous werewolf who's stalking his wife and child," I said, laughing. "That's exactly what it's like."

"You don't know anything," Eric said. "Maybe it was about money for a little while. But then he started to threaten me, threaten my wife, my daughter—"

"Okay, okay," I said. "Fine, you're under duress. So, what happened last night?"

"Well, Thomas was furious." Eric's eyes were wide, flitting back and forth between Jed's teeth and me. "He was looking to take his anger out on something. Or someone. And after going around in circles for a while, like – chasing his own tail—"

"Har har," I said.

"—he decided that all of this was his dad's fault." Eric's gaze settled on me. "All of it. That if he hadn't made Thomas a werewolf, none of this would have happened. Not the divorce, not the estrangement from Derrick...none of it." Eric licked his lips.

"Yeah, I'm sure it's all the wolf that's making him a dickhead," I said.

"I know, he's always kind of been that way," Eric said. "But not as much. And once he started talking about it – man, he's so proud of being a werewolf. Like...it's a big deal to him, a major part of who he is and there are traditions and stuff he's really into." Eric was just going now, no need to even prompt him with threats of Jed. "But he's so angry about his life going to crap that he was just looking for someone to blame. So he dragged me along to go show his dad that he was the stronger of the two of them. And that even though he was cursed, that he was still...I don't know, the alpha or something."

"Power struggle like whoa," I said.

Eric nodded. "And then, after we left – I couldn't bear to watch – he was on a high. He kept saying how his son was going to be strong, too. He kept talking about finding him, about passing on his legacy."

My face started to burn. "He's been chasing Derrick for days. Stalking him, really. He's relentless."

"Well, yeah. And he isn't going to stop until he gets what he wants," Eric said.

"Which is…?" I asked.

Eric blinked up at me. "You...you don't know why Thomas is after Derrick?"

"I heard the legacy talk from him," I said. "I have a suspicion. But I want to hear you say it."

"It's exactly what you think," Eric said, his eyes wide. "He wants to win him back in a way that will make sure he can't ever, ever go back to his mom, really. To put a block between them that she'll never be able to conquer because he'll always understand his dad better after he's been turned."

I closed my eyes for a second. There it was, the word I'd been dreading.

"He wants to make a man out of him," Eric said and my heart skipped a beat. "He wants to turn Derrick into a werewolf."

Chapter 27

I had to literally drag Jed off the top of Eric. Drool was dripping down, covering his eyes and the growls were frantic and loud. Jed wasn't happy with me, but I put my arms around his neck and pulled and pulled and he didn't resist too much.

"Thank you," Eric said, wiping his face with a hairy wrist. It didn't do much good, but he did it again a moment later because what else could he wipe it with? His scrubs were short sleeved. "Please just…get Thomas some help, will you? He may be completely insane right now, but…he's my friend. I don't want to see him suffering like this."

Jed snarled and I gave him a dangerous look. He didn't quail away, but it looked like he was mostly in control of himself. He kept both eyes on Eric, though.

"I'll do what I can," I said. "But I can't promise anything. My first priority is protecting Derrick. You know that, right?"

Eric took a deep breath, puffing out his cheek as he exhaled. "Yeah. That's fair." He glanced over at Jed. "And you don't need to worry about me reporting this or anything. All…this—" he said, gesturing to Jed. "No one would believe me, anyway."

I smiled at him. "I know these feels all too well."

I said goodbye and then watched him walk back toward the clinic. He was still wiping his eyes and I had a feeling he really needed a towel.

"All right, you, time to change back into a human," I said to Jed.

He turned his big, wolfish head up to me and his eyes narrowed.

"Come on," I said. "We don't have all day. We need to go back and get your hat and shoes. And then make our exit before animal control shows up. I mean, I assume it's animal control that shows up when you get out of control. Either way, the last thing you need is to be darted and put in a kennel."

Jed made a whine.

"Look, we can't have you roaming Clearwater as a werewolf," I said. "They probably have leash laws here, you know. And I'm definitely not picking up your crap. I don't have a bag or a scoop."

He bared his teeth.

"Fine," I said, rolling my eyes. "I was kidding about the last thing. But not the leash laws. Look at the size of you."

He let out one last whine and his body started to shrink, the fur starting to recede back into his skin and the size of his head returning to normal. His shirt was a torn mess, fur disappearing beneath it to reveal pale flesh. Same with his pants, where they'd caught beneath his feet. He had holes in both knees now, was covered in dirt and his hair was standing up at every angle. His suspenders were hanging on strong, though.

"I could get back a lot faster if I stayed a wolf," he said, glaring at me.

I glared back at him. "And what about me?"

He hesitated and his cheeks turned pink.

"And another thing," I said, as I started back toward through the trees. "What were you thinking taking off after him like that in the first place?"

"We had to question him, didn't we?" Jed asked, shoving his hands in his pockets. "I was just trying to help."

"Staying a human would have been the smarter thing to do," I said. "Half the county probably saw a werewolf bounding down the sidewalk, chasing after this poor man."

"Who cares what other people think?" Jed asked, noticing a low hanging branch, easily ducking underneath it and straightening up on the other side.

I turned on him and prodded my finger into his chest,

accidentally poking it through one of the tears in his shirt and against a thin layer of chest hair. I ignored this contact. "That is downright stupid thinking," I said. "I thought that part of your people's werewolf mantra was keeping to yourselves."

Jed frowned at me, his brow knitting together across his forehead.

"Your dad wouldn't exactly be happy with that kind of attitude, right?"

At that, Jed rolled his eyes.

"Oh, please," I said. "Don't go all rebellious teenager on me now."

Jed stormed passed me, huffing. His angry snort sounded like a dog's exhale. Seeing all these characteristics of the wolf in him, I started to wonder just how close to the surface this werewolf really was. Derrick's dad was certainly keeping his wolf up top, given how close he'd come to transforming right in the middle of our scuffle yesterday.

I rolled my eyes again and followed after him. "I agree we needed to catch him and I can see why you chasing after him as a wolf might seem like the better option at first—"

"It was the better option," he said simply.

Anger flared and I glared at the back of his head. "No, it wasn't." I said. "If you hadn't been so impatient, we could've saved ourselves all of this trouble of having to walk back to the clinic so we can get your shoes and hat."

Jed's face was reddening steadily throughout our entire argument and his jaw was clenched. Still, he said nothing.

"You barked at him right out of the gate, before we even left the clinic," I said. "When you shouted at him in the hallway. If you hadn't done that, escalating things, we could have asked him a couple of questions, gotten the information and left. No chase, no wolf, no need for the good cop, bad cop thing."

He gave me a confused look. "What are you talking about?"

"You, snarling in his face, scaring him half to death," I said. "Without him freaking out, it wouldn't have been necessary."

"Nuh-uh." Jed shook his head.

"What?" I asked.

"You just don't understand."

"What don't I understand?"

"What it's like to be a werewolf."

"I don't have to understand being a werewolf to know that you shouldn't just change into one willy-nilly thinking that your strength is going to be the answer to all of your problems," I said.

He didn't like that answer, based on his pupils dilating as he looked right at me.

"I get that you're eager to help," I said. "I get that you were doing what you thought was right. But that doesn't mean it *was* right. And that doesn't mean it wasn't reckless."

He didn't look at me, didn't reply.

"Right?" I asked, watching the side of his face.

He still didn't answer.

Ahead, across the street, I could just make out the ugly, seventies-style clinic where Jed's stuff remained. Jed walked a few paces ahead of me, his hands in his pockets, his shoulders hunched over. Pouting, probably. Or maybe I'd been too hard on him.

I felt a vibration in my pocket. Worrying that it was Mom calling, somehow discovering that I left school, I quickly pulled it out.

It was Derrick's number on the caller ID.

Jed, who heard the noise, turned around, watching me with his brows furrowed.

"Hello?" I asked, answering it. My heart rate had already started to increase.

"Cassie?" He was whispering and his breath came in short, quiet little gasps.

"Derrick?" I asked, my heart thundering. "What's the matter? Where are you?"

"It's my dad," he said under his breath. "My dad – he's here!"

Chapter 28

Jed glanced sidelong at me as we bumped along in the back of the Uber. "What do we do about Thomas when we get there?" he asked. His voice was low, but strained and he wouldn't look me in the eye.

"We have to protect Derrick and his mom," I said, fanning myself. The car's AC was struggling against the Florida heat and winning, by a little. Cool air was prickling my skin all along the sweat paths that had been carved across it by the endless trickles I'd experienced today. "That's the main priority."

"So, we should probably kill Thomas, right?" he asked.

My heart leapt into my throat at the same time the driver spun his head around to stare, horrified, at Jed. I guess he'd heard, in spite of Jed's attempt to keep it on the downlow.

"Video game boss," I said, cringing and realizing that this was another lie, dammit and it had popped out so easily. "He's talking about a..." I looked sideways at Jed, with his Amish hat and suspenders. "A video game. You know, because he's not allowed to play at home."

"Ohhhh," the guy said, nodding, a little grin on his face and a twinkle in his eyes. "I hear you, bro," he looked right at Jed. "My parents were strict, too, growing up. Probably not as bad as yours, but still. I feel you, man."

I waited until the driver had turned back around. "No," I said, lowering my voice while I shoved my elbow into Jed's ribs. "No, we're not going to kill anyone, Jed, you jackwagon." I shot him a death glare. "Why would you even suggest it?" I asked, the silly smile on my face mismatching the heat of my words.

He shrugged. "That's probably what my dad would suggest."

"No way," I said. "Your dad would never—"

"How do you think we enforce pack discipline?" Jed asked, leaning in closer to me so the driver couldn't hear. "The stakes of one of us getting loose and causing problems? They're real high. There have to be consequences on us, because the responsibility of this power is hefty. And it can't be just be shunning."

I blinked. I hadn't really thought about how the Amish would control the pack. "How...does that work?"

"Anything we do as wolves that we can't as humans?" He looked out the window. "It's allowed."

"Wait...so how much control do you have as a wolf?" I asked.

"Not total," he said, not looking at me. "But enough, most of the time."

I thought about that for a second as the driver brought the car to a halt. "Here we are," he said, way too chipper. "I wish you the very best of luck slaying the dragon or whatever, bro." He grinned at Jed.

"Yeah, I'm sure it'll be an epic boss battle." I shoved Jed toward the door.

"Hey—" he said scrambling for the door handle.

"Come on," I said, trying to put some urgency into it.

I jumped out of the car a second after him, slamming the door. We both stared up at Derrick's house as the car pulled away from the curb.

"Damn," I whispered, sweating again already. My hair hung in tangles around the sides of my face, drooping in the humidity.

The door was kicked in and dirty footprints covered the pristine white washed front porch.

We were too late.

Chapter 29

I hurried up the steps, throwing myself inside the house, staring around. My heart was hammering so hard against my chest, pounding against my eardrums.

I saw that things were off. A paisley-patterned arm chair was crooked. The corner of the rug was turned over. A tea kettle was whistling somewhere farther in the house.

On the coffee table, I saw a mug with a pink lipstick stain that was half full of coffee, the liquid still steaming. A cell phone sat beside it.

Jed right behind me, we pushed farther into the house. I pressed my fingers to my lips, telling him to be quiet. He nodded.

I could see the screens and white metal supports of the lanai out the French doors in the back through the dining room. The dining table that could easily seat ten was in place, flawless. That all looked normal. Silence reigned, other than a television babbling in the room we'd just passed through and the whistling of the teapot in the kitchen.

I followed that sound with my gaze, saw the opening to the kitchen was just off to the left…and I gasped.

Corinna was slumped against the flawless, white kitchen island, a trickle of blood rolling down her forehead from her hairline.

I hurried to her, hitting my knees against the hard grey tile as I landed beside her. "Corinna?" I gently touched her shoulder.

Jed came into the kitchen behind me, then stalked through the doorway to another room along the wall, shoes barely making any noise as he went.

Corinna opened her eyes, drawing in a deep breath. She looked right at me and gasped, from peaceful to panicked in a hot second.

"Easy," I said, grabbing her hand. "It's okay. It's me, Cassie. Derrick's friend."

Her eyes were glassy for a second, but as she blinked, they cleared. She focused her gaze on me. "Cassie?" Her gaze sharpened. "Cassie, oh, thank God you're here. Tommy – he took Derrick! He—"

"Slow down," I said. I stood up and pulled the screaming kettle off the cook top on the island and turned the burner off. "Take a few deep breaths, get your bearings."

Corinna was panting, her hand over her heart.

I opened the fridge and found a bottle of water. I also grabbed a kitchen towel with shaking hands, running it under some warm water in the sink. She might need that wound on her head looked at. I used to not do all that well with blood, but since vampires had become a regular attraction in my life, I'd sort of developed somewhat of an iron belly.

I sat down on the kitchen floor beside her, crossing my legs, passing her the bottle and damp towel.

She opened the bottle with fumbling fingers, downing half of it in three long sips. Then she pressed the towel to her forehead, exhaling heavily as a slow drip of diluted blood slid down her forehead.

Jed appeared from the entry again, eyes sliding around like he was hunting. He paused, looking around the entry points to the room and out the back doors. Even if I'd been about ready to strangle him back at the clinic, I was glad to have another set of eyes with me, watching my back while I helped Corinna.

My heart twanged as I realized that it should've been Mill...if he wasn't so stubborn in refusing to help me.

Well, that and it was the middle of the afternoon.

"All right, why don't you tell me what happened?" I asked.

She pulled the towel away from her head, glancing at the

bright crimson splotch there and her cheeks paled.

"You said it was Thomas, right?" I said, hoping to draw her eyes to me instead of the towel. "Derrick called me. He said his dad showed up."

Corinna nodded, closing her eyes as she did. "Yes. He showed up about an hour ago. He was pounding on the door and Derrick and I locked it, refused to let him in. He got angry, he...transformed." She closed her eyes and composed herself for a second. "Then he broke the door down."

She pursed her lips together and I saw a glimmer of tears in the corner of her eyes. "He came right at me, knocked me down. Then he grabbed my leg and dragged me to the kitchen here." She squeezed her eyes shut as though trying to blot out the memory. Or maybe recall it more clearly. I don't know.

"It's okay," I said. "You don't have to go into details if you don't want to."

She shook her head slowly. "No, it's okay. He got me out of the way so I wouldn't be able to help Derrick. He dragged him out of the house, screaming and fighting, but all I could do was sit here. I couldn't see – I couldn't—"

"Don't try to move too much," I said. "I'm worried that you might have a concussion."

Corinna's eyes widened.

"It's okay," I said. "Just take it easy." I didn't know what else to say but that.

She sank back against the island.

"I'm guessing you lost consciousness," I said. "Thankfully, it doesn't look like you've lost too much blood."

"I don't care about me," she said. "I need to get my son back before …"

"I know why Thomas is after Derrick…" I said after a few seconds of silence. "And it isn't going to be easy to hear."

Corinna took another slow draw from her water bottle. "I know why Tommy is after him. He told me years ago what he wanted…" She looked up at me. "I'm sorry, Cassie. I wasn't exactly honest with you earlier."

"What do you mean?" I asked.

"I should have said something that day you were here," she said. "I should've said something to Derrick. I think he knew, but didn't want to believe... He's been denying it, I think."

"I'm not surprised," I said. Who wanted to contemplate their parent inflicting harm or a curse on them? Biting them? Because that's surely what it was going to take. "You can't blame yourself. You didn't know this was going to happen—"

"I should have prepared him better," Corinna said. "That was my responsibility as his mother, wasn't it? When Tommy showed up at the school, I should have taken Derrick and fled the state. But I was so afraid and didn't want to believe that it would actually happen, that Tommy might actually take Derrick away from me…"

She sniffed, dabbing at her head again with the towel.

"He tried to turn me, too, you know," she said. "Something else I should have told Derrick. He said we would understand each other so much better, that we could grow old together this way." She sniffed. "I told him he wouldn't live to be fifty as recklessly as he was going. I refused him. He…was angry, to say the least."

She swallowed nervously.

"Then I told him that he wasn't allowed to turn Derrick. That I wanted him to keep his…his other side from Derrick…and he hated that. He kept going on about passing on his legacy." She closed her eyes. "He said he wanted to make his own pack. Said he was tired of being alone. I told him over and over that he wasn't alone, that his curse didn't have to be what defined him. I mean, it's three nights a month. He was human most of the time…why did he let the wolf become all he thought about…?"

"It's okay," I said again. "I hate to keep asking, but do you have any idea where they could have gone?"

"No." She shook her head. "I'm sorry. I really wish I did, obviously."

Honestly, I wished she did, too. But there was nothing that I could do now. We were too late.

Jed was standing by the French doors, staring out into the backyard. At least he was keeping an eye out. How much had he heard? I assumed all, but he didn't act like he'd heard a word of it.

"Hold tight," I said, eyeing the wound on her head again.

"I'm gonna make a phone call."

"Wait, don't leave me," she said. "Please."

"Don't worry, I'm not going anywhere," I said. "I'll just…go in the other room here, okay? I'll be right back."

I slipped into a room just off the kitchen and found myself in an office. I pulled out my phone, pushing aside any more fears trying to creep in and opened my contacts. My finger hovered over the screen and then I just forced myself to press the name. That done, I held my phone to my ear and my breath caught in my chest as I pictured the conversation ahead.

"Hello?" he answered.

"Hey, Dad," I said, starting to pace back and forth across the office.

"Hey, kiddo, what's going on?" he asked.

"Are you at work?" I asked.

"Shift's over. I just left," he said. "Why?"

"Well…I have a favor to ask," I said. I chewed on my lip.

"O…kay," he said. "What have you gotten into now?" Ouch.

"I—" I bit my tongue. *Don't lie, Cassie*, I thought. *You're done lying.* "One of my friends is in trouble. His dad – the guy from the thing at school – has kinda gone off the rails. He broke into his kid's house, attacked the mom and she's hurt pretty bad. I'm worried she might have a concussion."

Dad was silent for a moment and all I could hear were the sounds of the car driving along the highway.

"She really needs your help, Dad," I said.

"Does this have to do with vampires?" Dad asked.

"No, actually," I said. "But please. I need you to come and look at her."

I expected him to challenge me, to scold me, to tell me to call an ambulance.

But instead, he said, "All right. Where are you?"

I rattled off their address.

"I'll be there in about fifteen minutes," he said after a moment. I figured he was putting it into the GPS. "I'll do what I can, but if she's hurt beyond my ability to help, I will have to bring her into a hospital, okay?"

"Yeah, but if she can avoid telling doctors *why* she got hurt, that would be best," I said.

"Oh, great." He sighed and I was amazed, again, that he didn't press for information. "Keep her comfortable and conscious. Tell her that help is on the way."

"You're the best, Dad," I said, relief seeping through me, like a warm cup of tea on a cold day. "Thank you so much."

"I expect an explanation later," he said. "I love you."

"I love you, too," I said.

And we hung up. I returned to the kitchen and found Corinna scrolling through her phone. "I just got off the phone with my dad. He's a doctor," I said. "He's on his way over here to help you."

She gave me a skeptical look. "Wait, does he know—"

"Oh, yeah," I said, nodding. "He's in the know."

She sighed. "All right."

I smiled at her. "We're going to find Derrick, okay?"

"I'm sure you will." She frowned at me. "I just hope it's in time. I mean, how do we know that he hasn't turned him already?"

A sharp needle of worry lodged itself in among all of the other worries I was carrying right now. "I...don't," I said. "But we can't think like that now. It's best if we all just believe he's fine until something else proves us otherwise. Right?"

I heard a scoff and looked up to see Jed still staring out of the window.

I glared at the back of his head for a second before turning back to Corinna. "Can I get you anything? Maybe a pillow? Blanket?"

"I'm fine," she said, her eyes still a little blurry, but focused on me. "Just...please. Find my son."

"I can do that," I said, lapsing into a silence that I tried to make sound unworried.

What if Derrick was turned when we found him? What would happen?

A family would be ruined, that's what. A vicious werewolf would have succeeded in his goals and who knows how Derrick would be? He wouldn't be himself anymore, that was for sure.

As I tried to plan for what to do next, I found myself hoping that Derrick was good at stalling. And that he believed that the cavalry was coming.

Chapter 30

The silence in the Bauer house was getting pretty heavy when I wandered over to Jed. The TV was still talking, quietly, in the next room, the only break in an otherwise staggering noiselessness. Even the AC was deep in the background. Or maybe I was just deep in my thoughts.

"So your father's coming?" Jed asked.

"Yeah," I said. "He's a doctor. Should be able to help her." Jed sniffed in distaste.

"What?" I asked, the frustration that I had been feeling toward him growing again as if we'd never stopped fighting.

"You're wasting your time," he said, shaking his head. He kept his voice low, where Corinna couldn't hear. "And telling her stuff that ain't true. It's over. That kid is probably a werewolf by now."

"You don't know that," I said. I shot a worried glance at Corinna. Her head was back against the island and her eyes were wandering slowly around the room.

Jed shrugged. "Think about it. His father has made the decision. He's committed and he's been trying to get a hold of him for days now. Why would he wait?"

Anger flooded my veins and suddenly I felt a hot flush in my skin that had nothing to do with the Florida weather. "I don't know, okay? But I can't tell his mom that. She's having a hard enough time with all of this as it is."

"You should probably check her for bites," Jed said, nodding his head toward Corinna. "

I stole a glance at Corinna and lowered my voice even more. "You're kidding, right?"

Jed met my gaze with a knowing look. "Think about it. Man and wife are having problems. He feels like she doesn't understand him because he's a wolf." He arched his eyebrows, then looked at her.

"No," I whispered and then did a look of my own. I didn't see any blood anywhere on her, but Jed – knuckleheaded teen that he was – had inadvertently stumbled onto a very good point.

"I don't think he did," Jed whispered, "but we should make sure, because we don't want to be here when she changes. It's pretty gruesome the first time."

"Hey Corinna?" I asked, turning toward her. "Thomas didn't...bite you, did he?"

She blinked at me a couple times, then ran her hands over her body, a look of thinly veiled panic flashing across her chiseled features. After a moment's inspection she said, "No...no, I don't think so. I would know, wouldn't I?"

"Oh, yeah," Jed said, looking out the doors again. "It's not gentle."

"Way to panic her for nothing," I said, back to low whisper. "Why are you such a pain in the ass?"

"I don't know what you're talking about," Jed said sullenly. "And watch your mouth."

"It feels like you're working against me here, negative Nellie," I said. "Why are you so dead set to be a total drag in this?"

"I'm just being realistic," Jed said. "He's gone. You just have to understand that."

"I'm not giving up on him," I said.

"What if he wants to be a werewolf, huh?" Jed asked. "What's so terrible about being a werewolf?" Now I could see the anger, the wounding behind his eyes. We'd hit something here.

"There's nothing wrong with it," I said, trying to backpedal a little. "Is that what this is really about? I never said there was anything—"

"Your boyfriend hates werewolves," Jed said, his eyes

narrowing. "And you're talking about this happening to Derrick like it's the worst thing ever. I think you might have picked up an attitude from Mill."

"That's not true—"

"Feels true," Jed said, sinking further into the reaches of sullen. "You don't like my kind. Just like your boyfriend."

"He's a vampire," I said. "You guys have been enemies since the dawn of time. That's bad blood that goes back a lot longer than you or I have been alive." I paused. "Unless that feud actually did start with Jacob and Edward, in which case I guess it's a short history."

"Oh, it goes back further than some silly English book." He folded his arms across his chest.

"Look, I don't hate your kind," I said, trying to bring this back. "Maybe I don't understand you as well as I should. And that's on me, I guess, a little. But also on you guys, because you try and hide it. Which is fair. But that doesn't lend itself to an easy understanding for us outsiders. And if Derrick was choosing this path for himself – hey, I think I'd be okay with it. But he's not. So help me find him. Help me prevent any of this from happening, because I know you don't want any more rogues out there."

"I tried," Jed said. "You don't like my methods."

"Of course I don't. Your method is chasing people down and threatening them. Or worse, killing the rogues."

"I'll do whatever I have to in order to protect my pack," Jed said darkly.

I stared at him, baffled. "Even kill an innocent person?"

"You think Thomas is innocent?" he asked. "Look what he's done – here and everywhere else he's been. He came into your school, didn't he? Attacked his own father. The man's gone beast, slipped the leash that binds us in, keeps us *mostly* in control. He has no discipline and no reason to be disciplined, outside our code and our beliefs."

"I—" I said, my mouth going dry. "You're right, he isn't innocent, but you can't just go around threatening to kill people. That's not okay. Just like it's not okay to just turn into werewolf whenever you want."

"You are not my father," he said, glaring at me. "Who are

you to tell me what I can and can't do?"

"Are you listening to yourself?" I asked. "A breath ago you were talking about discipline and control, now you're willing to throw caution utterly to the wind. Your dad would freak out if he heard you saying these things—"

"Unlike my father, I'm incredibly proud of being a werewolf," he said. "I'm going to be a stronger and better leader of the pack than he ever could have been."

I stared at him.

"This…doesn't sound like you, Jed," I said. "Or your pack's ideals."

"There is a lot about us that you don't know," he said. "That you'd never understand. You and your secular ways— "

"Hey, I never said anything nasty about the beliefs that you and the rest of your pack hold," I said, pointing a finger at him. "I've been respectful to you and your family—"

"Respectful?" he said. "Showing up at our house, demanding that we intercede for you, come and fix your problems for you—"

"I have never *demanded* anything of you," I said, my blood surging with fire. "I came to ask for your help. You're werewolves, so who else would I turn to for help for my friend?"

"You barely know him," he said. "You're throwing yourself into harm's way for someone you barely know."

He was sounding too much like Mill and that was making me even angrier than I already was.

"Fine," I snapped, my fingers shaking with rage. "Fine. Then I don't need your help. Is that what you want to hear? Do you want to hear that I don't need you?"

"Yes," he said, his eyes narrow slits. "That's what I needed to hear." His hands balled into fists, he wheeled around and started toward the front door.

"What do you think you're doing?" I asked, a bite to my words, following after him.

"Leaving," he said.

"Is everything okay?" Corinna's voice sounded weak and she was watching him leave like I was.

"Yes," I called back over my shoulder.

Man, my not lying streak was taking a hit today. It has been zero days since last incident.

"Don't be an idiot," I hissed. "You're miles away from home."

"I don't care," he said, stomping out onto the front porch.

"How are you going to get home?" I asked. "You can't walk all the way back to Sarasota."

"I won't be," he said, stalking off the porch. I could see his ears lengthening as he went, the change already underway.

I glared at the back of his head. "Fine, go turn into a wolf, leave your shoes and hat behind. Men need those, not beasts. Hell, leave your suspenders, pants and shirt behind, too. Go ahead and walk away. Pout all you want, I'm not chasing after you."

He didn't say anything, didn't turn around.

He just turned into a wolf and bounded away at a run.

And I watched him go, a mixture of fury and sorrow filling my heart

Chapter 31

Dad's car was always messier than Mom's. His stainless steel coffee thermos was tucked into the cupholder, used, pale green stevia packets stuffed into the one beside it. He had quite the collection going. A crinkled brown bag peeked out from underneath his seat; apparently he'd made a fast food run for lunch someday that week.

His air fresheners were pine scented, but not the cheap ones. He said it helped to remind him of home in New York. It always smelled like Christmas to me.

"You want to talk about it?" he asked, after we'd been going a few minutes.

He'd treated Corinna pretty quickly, pronouncing her more or less fine, no concussion, surprisingly. That done, we'd gotten in the car and wordlessly headed for home. But the silence had only lasted a minute or so once we were in the car.

"Maybe. Thanks, Dad…" I said. "I was really worried about her."

"I held my tongue the whole time we were there," Dad said. "But I'd like to know what happened to her and what you were doing there."

I sighed, knowing how upset he was going to be when he knew the truth, but I had promised him that I'd tell him.

So I let him in on everything that had been happening in the last week. It was a long story boiled short, most of the emotion stripped out along with all the dangerous parts. A lie of omission, I suppose, resetting my "Days Without Incident" counter back to zero, but I consoled myself that at least it wasn't a bald-faced sort of lie.

We had stopped at an annoyingly long stoplight, cars whizzing by in front of us, as I finished my tale. "...and now I have no idea where Derrick is and I'm worried that when I finally do see him again, his dad will have turned him."

My father was quiet. He hadn't looked at me at all while I was talking. My heart was fluttering and I knew that he was disappointed.

He and Mom had said over and over, whether directly or indirectly, that they wanted me out of this supernatural stuff. They didn't mind Mill, though they weren't wildly enthusiastic about him and I think that Dad even sort of liked that I was friends with Iona. But it was still a touchy subject. And when we threw werewolves, witches and faeries into the mix? They'd just rather pretend none of it existed.

"You know, Cass..." Dad said.

Oh, great. Here it came. *The lecture.*

"Everything that you've been going through lately...all of the choices you've been making..."

A lump formed in my throat, making it hard to swallow. I tried to ready myself, emotionally, for what I knew was coming.

"You're...different now."

I blinked. That wasn't quite what I expected him to say. "What do you mean?"

"I know that Mom and I just learned the truth about everything, but...everything that you've been dealing with, the people you're helping, protecting..." He glanced over at me as a car honked at him somewhere behind us. The light had turned green. "You had to go through so much of it by yourself. Even still, you take on these things willingly and so bravely. I think that it's changing who you are."

It was...changing me? I guess that was true. I was a totally different person than I was when we moved down to Florida. Meeting Byron set me on a course that I never would've chosen for myself, but it had ultimately made me a better person.

He sighed. "You're growing up right before my eyes. I was

worried about you making friends and succeeding in school, maybe getting a boyfriend…and how horribly I'd handle that. But the choices that you've been making are those of an adult. Actually, you're making better choices than most adults I know. You're trying to help people instead of just trying to stick your head in the sand so you don't have to deal with what's going on around you."

My cheeks flushed and I looked down at the first aid kit. I was focused really intently on the sticker on the front that was peeling away in one corner. He was the only one who seemed to think that my decision to help Derrick was born of anything other than craziness.

"I really am very proud of you," he said in a tone that was making my heart squeeze. It was awkward and endearing at the same time.

"Dad…" I said in the most teenager way possible. *You're embarrassing me.*

"But I wouldn't be a very good father if I didn't warn you…" he said as we turned onto the road where our new temporary house was. "Being a doctor has allowed me to meet a lot of different people. I've met cowards and heroes. A lot of the EMTs have hero complexes when they first start, determined to make a difference, save lives. They're like crusaders. But they soon learn that it isn't all rainbows and sunshine. They see some grisly things, some things that will haunt you…and they get burned out sometimes. Even hurt. Those people either quit because they can't handle it, or they just harden their hearts to the pain all around them."

I understood what he meant. And he was right. I'd also seen some pretty gruesome things…things that gave me nightmares and made it hard to sleep.

"I don't mean to worry you or make you upset," Dad said. "I just want you to know that I love you and care about what happens to you. I want you to be safe. And I'm incredibly proud of you and how compassionate you've become. I think you're doing great things."

I really didn't know what to say. It was like I forgot how to work my tongue.

But I was saved having to reply as we pulled up to the house.

My eyes were drawn to dark objects against the white stucco front. There were two men in dark suits standing at the door. One of them stood out, dressed sharper than the other, like he was in Armani versus the other guy clad in something off the rack at Goodwill.

In the driveway where Dad normally parked was a sleek, black Jaguar that looked like it cost almost as much as Lockwood's new Maserati.

"Who is that?" I asked, sitting up straighter in my seat, brow furrowing as I stared at the men. They spared only a glance for us. Mom was there at the door, talking with them. She looked…subdued. Which was strange. I'd never seen Mom look sheepish like that.

Like she was cornered prey.

Chapter 32

The guy in the Armani-looking suit had a long, hooked nose, bushy black eyebrows and beady eyes. His face looked like he was born sneering and he could grate cheese on the wrinkles in his forehead if he wanted to.

The man beside him looked more like a rat, with wide front teeth, a squashed nose and watery eyes. His hair was thinning on the top of his head, which he had tried to comb over with the rest of his hair. The bag in his hands had the words *Private Investigator* stitched into the leather.

His eyes lingered on me a little too long and the smirk that followed made the hair on the back of my neck stand up.

"What's going on?" I asked Dad. I looked up at him and was surprised to see how pale he was, standing there in the driveway, staring at them.

In a flash, I realized he knew who they were. And he was not happy about it.

"Oh, this must be your husband. And your daughter?" Armani guy asked, as if he had just noticed us. "My goodness, she's pretty, isn't she? Just like her mother."

I moved to stand next to Dad, who was watching the men apprehensively. He wanted them to know that he was there, that he was watching and listening to everything that they did and said. He put his arm around my shoulders and pulled me close to him as we made our way up the front walk.

Armani gave Dad one of the fakest smiles that I'd ever seen and turned back to Mom, who was now seething, all trace of the fear I'd seen before gone.

"I hope you know that I'm making you a very generous offer," Armani said, his hook nose bobbling. It looked like it had been broken a time or two. Or maybe it was just malformed. He flashed a mirthless grin. "But it won't last forever. Because sooner or later, these clients of yours are going to know that you've taken advantage of them—"

Mom's eyes flashed and she straightened. "I don't need your help," she said.

"Oh, really?" said Armani. "What if your partners find out, hmm? You could lose your bar license. Be banned from practicing law ever again." He made an appraising look at the house. "You could lose..." He looked over at me. "Everything."

My skin crawled at his words. Who was this guy?

A nagging voice in the back of my mind made me ask myself about the possibility of them being right, that Mom did do something that could get her disbarred.

No way. Mom was such a stickler for ethics that she never would've crossed any lines like that...

Right?

Mom folded her arms across her chest. "Are you threatening my family?" she asked, her eyes flashing.

Oh, crap. They made her put on her lawyer face. This was not going to end well for them.

"Of course not," said Armani, laughing. He sounded like a monkey. "All we want is to help you right the wrongs that have been committed."

Mom's face colored. I could see it even from where I was standing in the driveway. The sound of some boys playing basketball down the street filled the uncomfortable silence between Mom and the men on the doorsteps, the steady echo of a basketball against concrete punctuating the silence.

"Yes, well..." she said uncomfortably. "Thank you for your time." She was not thankful. She was lying through her teeth. "Now, if you would please leave, it's dinner time and I haven't seen my family all day. Goodbye." And then she slammed the door in their faces.

The men registered surprise, but they weren't particularly

upset by it. They bent their heads together, whispering in voices so low that I couldn't hear what they were saying, then both turned and glanced at Dad and I, like we were intruders on their planning session.

"Come on," Dad said to me and he put his hand on my back, steering me toward the door into the garage.

The men watched us as we slipped inside and I was glad that Dad was with me. I'd have hated to use any of Mill's sweet martial arts moves on them given that they seemed human, albeit annoying. I debated asking him what the hell was going on, but the look on his face stopped me. He looked strained, like he had aged ten years in seconds.

Whatever those guys were here for had upset him just as much as Mom.

What in the world was going on with Mom? Did this have something to do with whatever she was trying to hide from me the other day? The stacks of files, the strain in her eyes…

And what did those guys mean about the clients who'd been taken advantage of?

What happened? What had she done?

Whatever it was…Mom was in deep.

Chapter 33

We stepped inside the house and I heard Mom scraping something from a skillet into the garbage can. There was a layer of smoke hovering near the ceiling, the smell of burned chicken and garlic heavy in the air and I covered my nose.

"Honey, what happened?" Dad asked.

Mom still had high spots of color in her cheeks as we entered the kitchen, and she was running the burned skillet under the tap in the sink. "Those...*men* showed up here," she said, scrubbing furiously at the pot with a steel wool scrubber. "They had the audacity to try and get me to file for—" She saw me standing there and clamped her mouth shut.

"What. I don't get to know why there was some scuzzy PI on the doorstep when I get home?" I asked, shrugging off my backpack and putting it on the ground. "And honestly, having *Private Investigator* printed on your bag? That's like me having *High School Student* on mine."

Mom ignored me. "Why do you have blood all over the sleeve of your shirt?" she asked, grabbing Dad's wrist. "And you, young lady." She turned burning eyes on me. "I got a call from the school today saying you ditched class. Where did you go?"

"She actually has a pretty good reason this time," Dad said, white knighting for me.

"Oh, really?" Mom snapped.

"My friend's dad is a werewolf, he kidnapped my friend and I was trying to find him," I said, not sure that would play out as a 'good reason', but at least it was true. "Dad helped me get his mom patched up after she was attacked."

Mom blanched. She opened her mouth to speak, but I jumped in first.

"I wanna know what's going on here, Mom. What did you do that could get you dis-barred?" I asked.

"It's none of your business," Mom said, starting to dab at the sleeve of Dad's shirt with a cold, wet paper towel.

"Honey, I thought you said that you had handled all of this," Dad said. I could hear an edge to his voice.

"I'm handling it," she said. "It's just taking more effort than I thought."

I frowned at the two of them. "Dad, you were just saying how much of an adult I was. How come I can't know what's going on with all of this? I'm a part of this family, too, you know. And with everything we've gone through together—"

"Obviously things are not handled," Dad said, also ignoring me. "A private investigator? That's serious. If they end up telling your partners—"

"They won't tell them," Mom said, letting Dad go and throwing the paper towel into the trash before returning to the skillet in the sink.

"Tell them *what*?" I asked. "Mom, I heard them say something about your clients and how you took advantage of them—"

"I—" Mom turned, pointing a soapy spatula at me. Some of the suds dripped off the end and hit the linoleum floor. "I didn't take advantage of them."

My eyes narrowed. "You just lied to me, didn't you?" Anger flared in me. "You can lie to me when you made *such a big deal* about me lying to you?"

"I did not lie," she said acidly. "I'm just not telling you the whole story."

"What did you do?" I asked. "Overbill them? Steal from them—"

I froze as Dad's face gave it away. His eyes widened and he glanced at Mom. And then he realized what he'd done. Mom was rubbing her forehead.

"Holy crap, Mom." I couldn't quite get my brain around this.

"You *stole* from your clients?"

It hit me like an avalanche. There were some things in my life that were constant and always were going to be constant. One, my parents were together and always would be. Two, I was the only child. Three, Dad was a doctor, Mom was a lawyer and they both were really good at their jobs. Mom and Dad were good people. They cared about others, they donated money to charities, they recycled, they never smoked and only drank alcohol on holidays.

And they didn't steal or cheat in any capacity.

"Cassie..." Mom pinched the bridge of her nose. "This is why I didn't want you to know. You don't understand."

The jig was up. I knew the truth. Finally, I knew the truth.

"How long?" I asked, my hands balling into fists.

"Cass—"

"How long?" I asked, even louder. "How long have you been stealing from your clients?"

She hesitated and I could see that she was fighting between being devastated and furious.

Fury won.

"Ever since the insurance company decided that having two house fires due to unsolved arson in two different states were suspicious enough to deny our claims," she said, unloading on me with one brief, devastating salvo.

Another kick to the gut. "Wait, what?"

Dad sighed, then nodded. "They denied our claim for the cost of the house repairs here in Florida."

"But it wasn't our fault," I said. "It was the—"

"The vampires," Mom said, a glint of burning, irritated triumph in her eye. "I know. But I can't very well tell them that, can I?"

There was a moment of silence as the truth settled over me. "So it was my fault..." I said, some of the anger fizzling out. "We're broke...and it's my fault."

"Cass, we've seen what those vampires are capable of," Dad said. "We know that you weren't the one who started the fire—"

"But if you hadn't gotten involved with them in the first place—" Mom said, talking over Dad.

"Like I had any control over it," I said, glaring at her. "Byron picked me, okay? I didn't go looking for him. He saw me and – whatever. I didn't choose this. Any of this."

"Cassie, we know that it wasn't your fault, but we're still in this situation because of these vampires setting fire to our homes," Dad said.

"You're lucky that no one in New York knew that it was you that started the fire at the nature preserve," Mom said. "Because we'd be in a lot deeper trouble if—"

"I've been doing everything I can to take on extra shifts so we can pay the contractors that are fixing the house in the time being," Dad said. He turned to Mom. "But I still can't understand why you felt the need to borrow from your clients—"

"I had it all figured out," Mom said, throwing the sponge into the empty sink and drying off her hands on a dishtowel as if she was trying to strangle it. "I was going to borrow the funds for a few weeks and put it back in after we had paid off all our debts and finalized the legal action with the insurance company—"

"Are you suing the insurance company, too?" I asked.

Mom rolled her eyes. "No, but I'm threatening it, because they can't just drop us on a 'feeling'," she said.

"Mom, this is insane, you know that, right?" I asked.

"It isn't insane if it is going to help us rebuild our house and keep being able to afford to feed you," she said, her eyes narrow, angry slits.

"But have you paid any of that money back yet?" Dad asked.

She rounded on him with a groan of frustration. "No, I haven't, because I had to pay the painters today."

"Okay, but do you have a plan to start putting that money back?" Dad asked.

"Of course," Mom said. "All I have to do is finish paying for the countertops and then I can start putting money toward it. It's going to be close, but I think—"

"You think?" Dad asked. "Hun, we can't have this be so uncertain. We have to—"

"I'm going to my room," I said, snatching my backpack off the floor and storming off towards the stairs. I was done. I couldn't stand hearing about any of this anymore.

"You haven't eaten," Mom shouted after me.

"Last I checked, you dumped dinner in the trash," I said before slamming my door behind me. I sagged against it, covering my face with my hands.

Mom was stealing from her clients. And it was all because of me.

As I sat there against the door, trying to keep myself from crying, Mom's voice carried down the hall to my room, angrier now than she had been before and soon after, I heard Dad's voice rise, too.

They continued their argument for some time and I listened to their anger flow out, free at last, no more need to hide it from me...until I couldn't stand listening any longer.

Chapter 34

I was grateful that my new bedroom was on the first floor. It made sneaking out way easier.

Darkness was falling over the world and I worried that I had lingered at home too long. I didn't want to think about the state that Derrick might be in. I had to go. I had to find him. And the only way that I could find him was for someone to give me a ride.

I'd texted Lockwood to come and pick me up. I had no intention of telling him what was going on with my mom, but that didn't mean that I couldn't fill him in on what was going on with Derrick.

My phone rang while I hurried down the sidewalk, heading for the next corner to wait for him. Sitting out in front of my own house would have been asking for hell to come raining down on me if my mom or dad happened to look out.

"So, we've caught the scent again?" Lockwood asked.

"Not yet," I said. "Unfortunately, his mom has no idea where his dad could have taken him. I'm literally back at square one. But I need you to come and get me."

"And do what, Cassandra?" Lockwood asked. "Drive around until we somehow stumble upon him and his father romping through the streets?"

I stayed silent. This sounded way too much like my argument with Mill. After the argument with my parents, I didn't need someone else to make me feel worse about everything than I already did.

"I talked to Mill," Lockwood said, almost like he read my mind.

"Oh?" I said, a flare of fear striking me through the heart. "What did he say?"

"That he's worried about you," Lockwood said gently. "That you're acting impulsively. That you're defensive and unwilling to listen—"

"Unwilling to listen?" I asked. "What about him? He hates that I'm spending any time with Jed. He's jealous."

"He is also worried," Lockwood said.

Partially hurt that Lockwood didn't immediately take my side, I pouted. "That doesn't make it okay."

"Perhaps not," Lockwood said. "He said that he apologized to you and you still walked out on him."

"What are you now, our counselor?" I asked. I was out of line, but I couldn't bring myself to care. I didn't need Lockwood and Mill on my back right now.

"I'm not trying to attack you, Cassandra," he said. "But you need to carefully evaluate what your next steps are. You're moving from having to be involved in this world to choosing to be involved. Are you sure this is the direction you want to go?"

I licked my lips, my mind racing for a clever reply. None came.

"I will do what I can to protect you, of course," he said. "Regardless of your choice."

"I don't need you to protect me," I said, but I regretted the words as soon as they were out of my mouth.

"Very well," he said.

I stared at the ground. I had pushed Mill away and now I was pushing Lockwood away. Were they both right and I was just unwilling to admit it? "Lockwood...I didn't mean—"

"I'm almost there. I'll pick you up on the corner." And then he hung up.

There was a pit in my stomach and my eyes stung.

What was happening to me? It felt like I was undergoing a transformation of my own, not unlike Jed or Thomas underwent when they became a werewolf. The tension at the edges of my life as I became...whatever the hell I was becoming, maybe an adult, like Dad said, it felt like it was going to tear everything apart.

Lockwood pulled up to the curb, pretending like nothing was wrong.

I wasn't too proud to apologize. "Lockwood?" I asked, hanging on the passenger door, leaning in.

"Hmm?" He looked across the seats at me.

"I'm sorry that I got so angry on the phone."

"It's quite all right," he said. "There's a lot going on. And I do trust you. I hope you know that. I've been able to count on you when I needed help. All that we're asking of you is that you trust us, too." His green eyes seemed to shine.

"Thank you." I needed to hear that just as much as I needed Mill's stubborn affection.

Someone cleared their throat and I looked into the Maserati's back seat to see Mill sitting there. "Hey..." he said, looking massively chagrined, as though I might explode at him. Again.

All the anger swelled inside of me, like helium filling a balloon. At him, at Jed, at my parents, at Thomas...And then, almost as it grew to an unbearable amount, it burst within me, fizzling out and I sighed.

"Hey," I said, staring down at the ground, still leaning on the open door. I was too scared to get in the car, too ashamed. I had acted like a child...but I really didn't want to have to admit that out loud, because compared to my little blowup at Lockwood, what I'd done with Mill was titanic by comparison.

I heard the soft *pat pat* of Mill's hand on the seat beside him, indicating that I should slide in beside him.

I swallowed nervously and shut the front door, opening the rear one. I hesitated there until the memory of Derrick came flooding back to me, along with the panic that I had been feeling for him all day, so I pushed aside my worry and slid into the car beside Mill. Once the door was closed, Lockwood pulled away from the curb.

"Do your parents know that you're out?" Mill asked. So quiet, so calm.

The scent of his bergamot cologne filled the car and I was surprised how calm it made me feel. He was wearing the black button up I had mentioned in passing once that I really liked and some dark washed jeans. He looked like a super model. A super model with a really big forehead, but hey, I thought he looked good. And that was all that mattered, right?

"No, they don't," I said, staring out the window. "When I left, they were arguing about…well, some things that are basically my fault. Again." It felt better than I expected to get that off my chest, like things got lighter.

"What do you mean?" Mill asked.

"Everything is my fault," I said, my emotions spinning out of control. When was the last time I had eaten? Or slept properly? These thoughts rattled at the edges of my consciousness as my feelings started to tumble out. "It doesn't matter what happens, all the choices I make inevitably come back to bite me in some way, even if they turn out for my good. Like, vampires being dead is good, right? But they ruined my life before they died and I still have to deal with all the crap they left behind."

Mill was watching me cautiously. Lockwood, too, was listening; I saw his bright green eyes glance at me every few seconds in the rearview mirror as he drove.

"And it's not in small ways, no. It's in big ways. Like running my family's finances into the ground. Pushing my parents to the brink, so they feel like they have to use unsavory means to make money, which puts us in even more trouble…"

Mill reached over and took my hand in his. I realized that I was actually still angry at him, but when I tried to pull my hand away from his, he held it fast. "Cassie…" he said, looking at me with his dark blue eyes. "I have to apologize. For the way I acted. You've been dealing with so much and I wasn't helping you like I should've been. I'm sorry for being a jerk. I'm sorry for hating on the werewolves. They're just so…rugged. And they always smell like wet dog."

Lockwood smirked from the front seat.

"And they're just so…Amish," Mill said.

Part of me wanted to pick up our fight right where we had left off. I was already in fight mode from my argument with my parents. But I didn't have the strength to. That and I really just wanted something to go right today.

"It's okay, Mill…" I said. "I'm sorry too. For acting like a stuck-up teenager who really has no idea what it's like to have lived the life you have or seen the things you've seen."

He gave me a searching look. "Well…that was a very mature apology. I don't think you're stuck-up, I think that you were right to challenge me for my attitude. I understand all you wanted to do was help your friend…and that I wasn't there for you."

Lockwood smiled again from the front seat.

"What is it, faerie boy?" Mill asked. "Why are you so happy up there?"

"Oh, nothing," he said, but the smirk was lingering on his face. He was meddling. Acting like my faerie godfather.

"So, what now?" Mill asked, squeezing my hand. "Lockwood gave me a very brief overview of what's been happening. Fill me in."

I told him everything that had been happening for the last forty-eight hours. I watched a smirk pass over his face for only a second when I told him about my fight with Jed, but it was gone in a flash and he didn't push me about it.

"…And then I showed up at home and there were these two weird guys at the front door, talking with Mom. I knew there was something up with her, but I've been so worried about what's going on with Derrick that I didn't find out what until tonight. And let me tell you, it's a doozy—"

"I hate to break up the conversation," Lockwood said, doing just that. "But I thought that I should let you know…"

"Know what?" I asked, my heart skipping a beat.

His green eyes flitted in the rearview, looking past Mill and I. "We're being followed."

Chapter 35

At the sound of Lockwood's warning, I whipped around in the seat and peered out of the back window into the fallen night. Headlights peered back at me in the gloom and past them, I couldn't see anything.

"Lady Cassandra, be careful," Lockwood said. "They'll see you."

I squinted into the dark and I still couldn't see past the headlights of the car behind us. "Take the next turn," I said. "And then the one after that. Let's see if they actually are following us."

"That's what I have been doing," Lockwood said, but still flicking on the turning signal and making the right turn at the light. "Four times now. Unless this is some strange coincidence…"

We passed under a streetlight and I watched hard as the car following us was flooded with rays of light a few seconds later.

And the tiny hairs on the back of my neck stood up straight as I saw the silver jaguar hood ornament gleaming in the bright light.

I sunk back down on the seat with a groan.

"What?" Mill asked.

"I know who's following us," I said.

"Who is it?" Lockwood asked.

"That scummy lawyer and private investigator that were at my house this afternoon," I said. "The ones that accused my mom of malfeasance." I frowned. "Why are they following me? They wouldn't actually be trying to, like…kidnap me or anything, right?"

Lockwood's fingers were gripping the wheel. "I wouldn't think so, no. Even if they are unsavory, surely they wouldn't stoop to that level."

"Why were they at your house?" Mill asked.

"Mom's been stealing money from her clients," I said, glancing over my shoulder again to see if they were still following us. Of course they were.

"Your mother doesn't exactly strike me as someone who would do that," Mill said.

"She's not," I said. "But she didn't have enough money to cover the fire damage to our houses here and in New York—"

"Issues with the insurance company?" Lockwood asked.

I nodded.

"And now these guys are following you?" Mill asked. He started to roll up one of his sleeves. "Well. I'll fix this."

My cheeks flushed at Mill's words. He wanted to protect me that much, huh?

"My guess is that their intentions are to find some dirt on your mother in order to increase their leverage. They will most likely want a quick settlement," Lockwood said.

"Wow, Lockwood," I said. "That makes sense. Still, this is really scuzzy."

"Agreed," Mill said.

I looked up at Lockwood. "Can we lose them?"

"I've been trying," Lockwood said. "However, I don't think this is their first circus."

"Their first circus?" I asked, arching an eyebrow at him. "Do you mean their first rodeo?"

Lockwood's green eyes narrowed and his cheeks turned pink. "Oops. Yes."

"Where're we heading?" Mill asked. "Do we even know where to start looking for Derrick and his father?"

I sighed. "No, I don't. And the only person who might have any idea would be his Mom and she had no idea when I was there just a little while ago."

"Perhaps you should try asking her again," Lockwood said.

"Dad told me to give her some space, though…" I said.

"Desperate times call for desperate measures," Mill said. "And I'm sure she wants to help in the search for her son."

"There is a chance Derrick has contacted her since you spoke with her last," Lockwood said.

"True." I pulled my phone out of my pocket and scrolled through my numbers until I found Corinna's, which I got before we left her house. I chewed on my lip as I waited.

"Hello?" She picked up after the fourth ring. I could hear the fear in her voice.

"Mrs. Bauer?" I asked. "It's Cassie Howell."

"Cassie?" she asked. "Did you find Derrick? Do you know where he is?"

"I was just about to ask you that same question," I said, my heart sinking. "Unfortunately, I don't know where he is. Not yet. But I'm looking. That's why I had to call you. I know my dad told you that you needed to rest, but there were a few questions that I had."

"Cassie, I really should keep this line open," she said. "I called the police already and—"

"You called the police?" I asked. I rolled my eyes. "Mrs. Bauer, you know that the police won't find anything. They wouldn't even know what to look for. They have no experience with werewolves."

"What was I supposed to do?" she asked, her tone turning from fear to desperation. "Just sit on my hands and hope that he'll just wander back in the front door?"

"No," I said. I was starting to get frustrated. "Not at all. It's just—"

"Cassie, I appreciate that you found me when you did this afternoon and that I'm not alone in all of this supernatural insanity. But I have to—"

"Mrs. Bauer, I get that I'm just a teenager sticking my head into something that doesn't really concern me," I said. "But Derrick is becoming a friend of mine and I want to be able to make sure he's safe, too. And the reality is that I might be the only one who can. So…can I ask you some questions?"

My question was met with silence on the other end of the line.

"Did I lose you?" I asked after a few heartbeats' worth of

quiet.

"No, I'm here," she said. "What are your questions?"

Good. At least she thought about what I said and didn't just immediately write me off.

"There's got to be a place where Thomas would take Derrick," I said. "A place that only they could go. Maybe a secret hideout? Or maybe a place where they would traditionally turn another werewolf?"

She was silent again.

"I know that we might be grasping at straws, here, but—"

"Tommy did say something once," she said quietly. "About the turning. It happened on his dad's farm."

I turned my eyes, wide with fear, to Mill who could hear the whole conversation.

"Okay," I said. "Thank you, Mrs. Bauer. I'll keep in touch."

"Wait, you don't think that Thomas would actually take him there, do you? Tonight?" The fear in her voice was threatening to unhinge me.

"I don't know for sure," I said. "But I have the cavalry in tow, so we'll get him, okay? Just don't worry about it."

Like she was going to listen to that.

We said goodbye and I looked up at Lockwood. "Old Man Bauer's farm," I said. "I should've known that was where this was going to end up."

"So, we're headed back to Sarasota?" Mill asked.

"Guess so," I said.

Lockwood's gaze was glued to the back window. "A grand tour, I suppose. Or perhaps a caravan."

"All right, this is getting ridiculous," Mill said. He looked over at me. "Do you want me to take care of them?"

"What do you mean, 'take care of them'?" I asked. I tried not to imagine him leaping onto their windshield, ripping them both out of the car before tearing their throats out.

"Just scare them off," Mill said.

"Not eating them?" I asked

He gave me a look. "I don't like the taste of scumbags."

I smirked. "Good to know."

"But seriously – do you want me to deal with them?" Mill asked.

I debated for a half a second and then sighed. "No. I don't want you to do anything crazy."

We settled into an uneasy silence as Lockwood turned the car yet again. The black Jaguar followed, of course and the longer they stayed with us, the more I started to regret telling Mill to leave it be.

Chapter 36

It was after eleven when we finally made it to Sarasota. Lockwood thankfully remembered the way to the Bauer farm and we continued down the long, straight stretch of road to the east after we got off the interstate.

I stared out of the window up at the sky. Living just north of Tampa meant enough light pollution that I never saw the stars anymore, or hardly at all. I saw a few particularly bright ones, but I missed the countless stars I was able to see back in New York. The moon overhead was full and brilliant. It made the fields around us look like they were glowing and I could see almost as clearly as I could during the day.

I nearly jumped out of my skin when a howl broke through the silence of the night. I grabbed for Mill's hand. I wondered for a second if it was Jed. There were a lot of other werewolves around, too. But Jed was surely out there somewhere.

An uneasy squirming in my heart came and went as I thought about Jed, about our fight. I wondered what he was up to right now. And, a little embarrassed, I wondered if he'd forgiven me.

"It is the full moon, isn't it?" Lockwood said, glancing up. "Caution is advised, then."

The closer we got to the farm, the more howls we heard in the distance, over the smooth purr of the Maserati.

Mr. Armani suit and his creepy compadre were still following after us, something that Lockwood felt I needed to be reminded of every ten minutes or so. They were hanging back as we turned onto the long drive that led to the Bauer farm.

Lockwood stopped the car a ways back from the house and barn, his headlights flooding the dirt driveway with light. The edge of the forest that the farm butted up against was filled with shadows. It was eerie, like something out of a horror movie. The trees swayed in the wind, like bony fingers scraping against the sky overhead.

The farmhouse was dark and quiet. The barn door was slightly open and a metal bucket was just outside in the dust, lying on its side, the contents having splashed all over the ground. Something had kicked it over and didn't care to stop and pick it up. Another gust of wind sent it rolling, tumbling across the rough ground like a tumbleweed in an old Western.

One lone echoing howl filled the night and I was glad that we were inside the car still.

"That one was close," I said just above a whisper.

Mill's face was hard as he stared out into the night. "Yes."

A few more answering howls were heard from somewhere farther in the distance.

"We should go," Lockwood said. I saw a flicker of green light from between his fingers. Something magical. He was preparing.

"He's right, we won't find Derrick sitting in here," Mill said, but there was a tightness in his voice that made my stomach queasy.

Quietly, all three of us got out of the car. I pushed the door shut silently, then bumped it close with my hip to avoid making noise. The warm air washed over me, brushing some of my hair out of my face. Even with the heat a chill washed over my skin. That werewolf was close. And I couldn't see anything outside of the field of light from Lockwood's headlamps, which he'd left on for us.

Mill walked around the back of the car to stand beside me. His closeness made me feel a little safer as I stared around into the dark.

"Look," he whispered to me. "I know you like these Amish. They seem sweet to you, or whatever. But if they catch us here tonight, during the full moon, they will rip us to shreds."

A lump appeared in my throat. So the full moon really did make them all crazy. Why did Thomas have to steal Derrick away during the full moon? Why couldn't it have been when the other werewolves were nice and calm and not stalking around in the darkness, just beyond the reach of the shadows?

I jumped as I heard what sounded like an animal padding across the grass from somewhere in the shadows.

Mill moved between me and the sound.

"Lady Cassandra," Lockwood whispered from the front of the car. "Come here."

Slowly, I made my way over to him, keeping my eyes glued to the darkness, to the empty farmhouse, to the open barn door. Something was going to pop out at me and scare me half to death, I just knew it.

"Thomas is about," Lockwood said, pointing to a patch of complete blackness behind the farmhouse. "He is watching us. He's protecting—"

And then I saw him. Just before the tree line, there was a tall, thick pine tree that was surrounded with round, flat stones and sand. It was almost like an altar.

But that wasn't what surprised me. It was the fact that Derrick was tied to that tree, his arms wrapped all the way around to the back. He was doubled over, his chin lolling against his chest.

"Lockwood, you don't think he's—" I said.

Another howl rent the air and my nerves burned like electric currents were coursing through my veins.

Derrick's chin snapped up at the sound and I gasped.

His eyes went wide, wild and terrified. He'd been jarred awake by the howl. His blond hair was sticking to his forehead, his face shining with sweat. Teeth gritted, jaw clenched, he was straining at the bindings behind his back.

"Cassie?" he gasped, spittle flying out from between his lips. "What are you doing here?"

I cautiously moved toward him. "I came to get you, Derrick."

"No, Cassie," he said, desperation coating his words.

My skin began to crawl.

"I'm not leaving you here," I said. "I brought help. We're

going to—"

"Go, Cassie, go!" Derrick said. "Now, go!"

A low, deep growl sounded from right behind me. I could almost feel breath on the back of my neck. The gravel crunched on the ground beneath my feet as I turned to look over my shoulder.

And was met with the face of a werewolf.

Chapter 37

"Cassie!"

I wasn't sure if it was Mill, Lockwood, or Derrick shouting at me. Maybe all three of them at the same time.

The werewolf, who I could only assume was Thomas, plowed me down as easily as if I were a young child. I hit the ground with a thump, all my weight landing on my back, plus that of the wolf. My head rang and the stench wafting off of him made my eyes water and bile rise to the back of my throat. The shock of being knocked over faded immediately, adrenaline driving me back to panicked alertness.

Thomas raised his clawed paw that looked like it was the size of a manhole cover. It rose slowly, as if to bat into me like a punch and just as he brought it down, he disappeared from my view with a *thud*.

I looked to my left at the sign of movement and saw Mill land on top of Thomas some ten feet away, the two combining in a tangled mess of limbs. Mill had moved in a blur to tackle him off of me and the snarling they produced was terrible. Mill had him pinned, but Thomas's long teeth were gnashing at my boyfriend. Mill's own fangs were bared, but his strength was clearly matched by Thomas's.

"Cassandra, quickly—" Lockwood said, summoning an orb of blue flames in his palm. "Tend to your friend."

I shook my head and scrambled over the dead leaves and dry grass to Derrick.

Thomas howled and then Mill shrieked in pain, causing my

fingers to go numb and a pain as cold as ice to consume my chest.

"Cassie, you can't," Derrick said, struggling in vain against the bindings behind him as I approached. "You have to—"

"Shut up," I said, my fingers trembling as I examined his back. It was so dark that I could barely see anything and the noises coming from Thomas and Mill's fight was driving me insane. There was snarling, the thumping of a body against the hard earth and cries of pain.

I couldn't see any of it from where I stood behind the tree.

Pulling my cellphone out of my pocket, I turned the flashlight on and pointed it to Derrick's bound wrists.

More piercing howls from distant werewolves came from the forest behind me, causing me to drop my phone in fright as I looked wildly around for the source. I whipped around, trying to recognize any flicker of movement in the dense trees, or to hear the snap of a twig or the rustle of leaves.

I didn't hear any, so I hunched down and picked up my phone from the grass. A whoosh and a burst of blue light back at the fight between Mill and Thomas told me that Lockwood had gotten involved.

I was panting, staring desperately, hopelessly at the rope that tied Derrick to the tree. I'd never seen a knot like it before. It was tight and complicated and obviously one of those knots that seemed to get tighter the more Derrick struggled.

"Are you okay?" Derrick asked, still pulling against it.

"I—" I said, my voice shaking. "I don't know – I don't know how to free you—"

"Don't worry about me," Derrick said. "Just go! Get back to your car, get out of here!"

I tried to take a steadying breath, ignoring the throbbing adrenaline in my head, the way my body twitched at every sound that came from the fight such a short distance away. I peered out from behind the tree and saw their silhouettes in the light from the Maserati's headlamps.

Thomas was a beast. He moved as gracefully as Mill did and kept pace with him. They were spinning and striking, a ballet of death. But where Mill was strength and precision, Thomas was feral savagery. The fight was brutal and I was frozen to the spot, unable to look away.

Derrick. I had to free Derrick.

But Mill…

Thomas's claws dug deep gouges in the ground beneath him. Mill's foot caught one, causing him to stumble. He managed to break free from Thomas's grasp, but as he turned to strike, Thomas met him with a swift pounce. Mill was fighting like a person. Thomas, like an animal.

He struck out with his clawed paws, catching Mill in the arm and then dove at him with teeth extended, latching onto Mill's collarbone with his wide jaw.

"No!" I shouted, my hands clapping to my mouth, all thought of freeing Derrick forgotten.

Mill tumbled to the ground and when Thomas finally let go and I could the droplets of black blood dripping from Thomas's teeth. Mill lay exactly where he landed.

My body was taut, my hands clenched into fists, my mind zooming by at a million miles a second. I was about to bolt over to Mill, not caring even a little that Thomas was still there, hovering over him, breathing over his body, when Lockwood's silhouette appeared, lighting up the space between them with another orb of bright blue light.

Mill moved, too, rolling over onto his side. I could barely see him in the shadows outside of the brightness from the headlights.

"Dad, stop!"

I came to my senses, wheeling around to see Derrick pulling and yanking his arms, apparently forgetting that ropes and a tree held him in place.

"Don't hurt them—" Derrick shouted.

I swallowed hard and hurried back around the back of the tree. My hands were steadied by urgency and purpose as I turned my flashlight back to the ropes knotted around Derrick's wrists. I could smell the metallic blood, see the raw skin underneath the rope where it had cut into his skin.

"Just hold on," I said to him. "I'll figure out a way to get you out of here."

Lockwood blasted Thomas with more magic, casting everything in an explosion of orange light. A howl of pain from Thomas told me it had been a direct hit.

I had no pocket knife and made a mental note to pick one up for situations like this where my friends were bound to trees. Mill's teeth would probably have worked, but he was down, maybe for the count. My stomach roiled nauseously at that thought.

Lockwood could probably cut it away with some magic, but he was a little busy at the moment keeping Derrick human and me alive.

My foot crunched the rocks beneath my feet and –

Rocks.

I turned my light down to the ground at my feet. Sinking down to my knees, I brushed my hand through the grass, looking for one sizable enough, one sharp enough to maybe do the job. I found one that was probably too smooth to cut through the rope, so I struck it against a gnarled root of the tree.

The soft stone shattered, leaving a jagged edge on one of the pieces. "That'll do," I said, getting back to my feet and pressing the stone to the ropes.

"What are you doing?" Derrick called over his shoulder as I started to hack away at the bindings.

"Getting you out of here," I said, my tongue between my teeth as I tried to get the jagged stone to saw through the thick fibers of the rope. "Very slowly, but still."

Three or four bursts of green light glowed beyond the tree and I heard Lockwood yell out in pain.

My face flushed as I tried to saw even faster.

The rope was resistant, but it was coming apart. Little fibers were fraying, twisting and standing up on their ends as I passed the stone over it again and again and again. It became hot in my fingers.

"Cassie," Derrick said nervously. "Your friends. They're—"

Another snarl from Thomas reached me behind the tree.

It was breaking. I just needed to focus, to think of nothing else aside from this little stone and it would –

The rope gave and a burst of elation washed over me. I helped untangle Derrick from his bindings, tossing the rope to the ground. I hurried around the tree, glanced at Derrick, standing there rubbing his wrists, but my eyes were drawn to Thomas, who was sniffing Mill's body.

I could smell the acrid vampire blood from here.

I had Derrick free. Check. Done. Ten points to Gryffindor. But Mill and Lockwood...

Lockwood was dragging himself away, one of his legs bleeding. He had summoned some sort of golden light and was bathing his wound in it. But it wasn't working fast enough.

Because Thomas had turned his attention on us.

Thomas was still standing. How had he managed to take down both Mill and Lockwood?

We were trapped. Thomas was between us and the car, his head down, teeth slick and shining blood and gore from my two much more powerful friends. His eyes glinted in the dark, fixed on us. Even if Derrick and I made a run for it, I couldn't leave Mill and Lockwood.

I swallowed nervously, wielding my sharp, jagged rock. It wasn't even a handful, hardly even a weapon at all. But if he was going to strike, then I wanted to be able to hurt him, even a little, before he took me down.

And it looked like he was about ready to do just that.

Chapter 38

Movement out of the corner of my eye made me turn my head to the ground behind Thomas. Mill was dragging himself to his feet, black blood staining his neck and the side of his face.

Fear flooded through me, fighting against the relief that he was still conscious. Did that bite mean that Mill was going to become a vampire werewolf now? What would that look like?

Mill let out a nasty, terrifying cry and launched himself at Thomas's back. The wolf started to turn—

Lockwood's leg seemed to have mended enough, because he took the chance to toss a spell at Thomas just then. It was a sickly green color, almost like a ball of slime and it clung to Thomas's side after it struck, emitting a foul smell like an infection, distracting the wolf long enough for Mill to land on him.

Thomas didn't take that lying down, though. He managed to grab onto the back of Mill's shirt by reaching over his head, pawing at him and ripping him free. He slammed Mill down to the ground like a ragdoll.

The sound was bone-chilling and it made stars pop up in my vision. Had he killed Mill?

He tossed Mill aside, his attention moved back to us and he started toward Derrick and I again.

"Come on, we need to run!" I shouted, grabbing Derrick's hand and pulling him away from the tree.

But Thomas was not dissuaded. He bounded toward us, growling all the while.

171

I watched in horror as Lockwood threw himself between us, tossing up what I could only describe as a forcefield, the edges of the nearly clear spell sparkling with white light. Thomas struck the shield, but it disappeared quickly under the force of his attack.

Lockwood lifted his hand, all aglow with blue magic. He seemed to try to summon another one, yelling at me over his shoulder. "Get to the car!"

Thomas slammed into Lockwood, knocking him spinning out of the way. Lockwood smashed into the tree where Derrick had been tied up, then falling to the ground,. unconscious.

Derrick slowed, staring back at his dad. "Cassie, it's no use." Thomas was staring us down, growling.

"Come on, we need to—" I said.

"We can't do anything, he's too strong," Derrick said.

"We can't just stand here," I said, tugging his arm.

Thomas lifted his head and howled at the moon. The call was taken up by almost a dozen other werewolves still hidden in the dark somewhere.

"Uh oh." My blood ran cold, freezing me to the spot. I shoved Derrick aside and moved to stand in front of Thomas, who was slowly padding his way over to us, his long teeth bared, the blood from Mill's shoulder staining his maw.

I held out the little stone, knowing how futile it was, how stupid, how useless.

A bark echoed behind us and Thomas, Derrick and I looked around to see a copper colored wolf standing in the flood of light from Lockwood's still running car. Even from where I stood, I could see the blue of his eyes as he stared at Thomas.

I might not have recognized him on sight before, but after today, there was no mistaking him.

It was Jed.

His tail wagged anxiously, he was poised and ready to strike. He turned his angry gaze to me and my stomach dropped out from beneath me.

Mill's words floated to mind. *I know you like these Amish. They seem sweet to you, or whatever. But if they catch us here tonight, during the full moon, they will rip us to shreds.*

Would Jed hurt me? Was he in his right mind enough to know that it was me that Thomas was cornering? Would he even care?

Was Mill right? Was this just all going to end in a bloody fight? I didn't really like the idea of being pulled limb from limb…or becoming a werewolf, for that matter.

Jed and Thomas stared at each other for a moment and it was like an electrical current passed between their eyes. The growling grew more intense. With horror, I watched Jed spring, at last, into the air, over Mill, over the distance between us –

He was angry with me. Horribly angry with me. We'd argued, fought. Of course he'd remember that, it'd sit with him. He'd make me his target.

Did I deserve this, though? Did I deserve to die just because I upset him?

But those thoughts were wiped from my mind as he sailed over Derrick and I and landed with all four of his paws on top of Thomas.

It was a disgusting sound that rose from their fight. Snapping and yipping, growling and crying.

I grabbed Derrick and dragged him, unresisting, out of their way. They were fighting like rabid animals, flipping over one another, their paws flailing, their tails lashing. My heart was beating like a drum as we watched them bite at each other's limbs, draw blood and howl.

"We need to get out of here," Derrick said. "This isn't going to—"

But he didn't need to finish his sentence. The two had rolled into the shadows, but even in the dim light of the moon, I saw Jed get his wide jaws around Thomas's throat and –

The gasping, sputtering sounds emanating from Thomas told me that Jed had succeeded in ripping his throat out.

Derrick, who was standing beside me, arm wrapped around mine, slowly pulled away from me, his hands covering his mouth as he stared at the lumps of shadows a short distance away.

Jed growled, slowly climbing off of Thomas. Then turned his gaze on us.

Mill was suddenly there, between us and Jed, his arms spread wide. His footing was shaky and he couldn't hide the fact that his legs were trembling with the effort of staying upright.

"Mill—" I said.

"Get to the car," Mill said. "Now. Go!"

I stared at Jed over Mill's shoulder. The werewolf's tail was twitching, His paws were squared, ready to leap again.

But it didn't happen. He didn't. He didn't move, didn't even try to make a run at us. His tail relaxed and he gave Mill a wide birth as be began walking around us back toward the forest where he had come from.

"I – I don't understand—" Mill said through gritted teeth. "Why isn't he—"

"Who cares," I said, not wanting to argue, even though I knew why. "We need to go, now, while we can."

Mill nodded his head, turned and winced, his hand going to his collarbone and the movement brought fresh, black blood to the surface of his wound.

Derrick was there beside him in a second, putting his arm underneath Mill's to support him.

"I'll get Lockwood," I said, hurrying over to the downed fae.

Jed lingered near the tree, just outside of the car headlights. I knelt down over Lockwood, but I kept my eyes on him. He was barely moving, but his chest rose and fell with his breaths.

"Cassie, come on," Mill said, he and Derrick slowly struggling toward the car together.

I pulled Lockwood's arm up over my shoulder.

"Hm…what?" Lockwood said coming to. "Cassandra…why—"

"Come on, Lockwood. We need to go."

Lockwood's face screwed up in pain as he struggled to get to his feet, even with my help. It didn't help that he was a full-grown man of mostly muscle and I was just a teenage girl who really needed to stop skipping leg day. And arm day. And, again, cardio.

Lockwood and I started awkwardly making our way back to the car, but I shot a look over my shoulder once more at Jed. His eyes were boring into my back as I walked and my heart constricted in my chest, rising up into my throat.

It was *him*. He was aware of me, just as I was aware of him. He had saved us and had somehow maintained control of himself all throughout.

How could he? Mill had told me that werewolves lost their sense of themselves during the full moon. How had he managed to keep a clear head?

The blue of his eyes was intense. There was a curiosity there and something else, as I stared into his eyes.

"Cassie," Derrick said. He'd just helped Mill inside the car. "Come on!"

I shook my head, my cheeks burning as I looked away. I had shared looks like that with Mill a few times, but…it was almost as if Jed had seen right into the very core of me…

And had found something in me worth saving.

Chapter 39

Since everyone else in the car was recently injured, as the least wounded party I took the driver's seat in the Maserati. I knew Lockwood would kill me for switching all of his settings, like pulling the seat up so I could actually reach the pedals, or moving the rearview mirror so I could see out of the back window, but hey, he wanted to make it off of Werewolf Farm in one piece, right?

Derrick was up in the passenger seat next to me, staring out of the window into the night as we made our way back up the dirt driveway to the Bauer farm, looking like a deer in the headlights. The Maserati was very intuitive. And smooth. Too bad Mom and Dad were having money problems, because this would have been a very nice birthday gift for me.

I glanced in the backseat as we went over a particularly nasty bump in the driveway, hoping that Lockwood wasn't going to reprimand me too much for it and saw Mill checking Lockwood's head for wounds.

He caught me staring at him in the mirror and I immediately looked away, my cheeks turning bright red.

Had he seen the way that Jed had been staring at me? Was his jealousy that had made me so angry this whole time actually justified?

No, that couldn't be. Jed had insisted that he didn't have feelings for me. And how could he? We barely knew each other.

"I don't understand what happened back there," Mill said,

pulling out a fresh gauze pad from the first aid kit that Lockwood kept on the floor in the backseat. He seemed to need one, given how often he drove me around. Mill dabbed at a particularly nasty gash over Lockwood's eyebrow, his silver blood trickling down his nose.

"What do you mean?" I asked. I could see the main road ahead, streetlights glinting in the night.

"I didn't think that a werewolf was capable of that kind of thing," he said. "Completely going against their predator instinct to protect someone."

"He probably hated Thomas more than he wanted to eat us." I swallowed nervously. "I mean, he was against Thomas from the very beginning," I said. "Said it wasn't right that he wasn't part of the order…stuff like that."

Mill was quiet for a moment. "I don't think so. I'm willing to eat my words. Not every werewolf is murderous and insane."

"That's very big of you," I said.

We pulled out onto the road and I breathed a sigh of relief. Real asphalt, lights overhead. We were on our way home.

"Are you okay?" I asked Mill, wanting to change the subject to spare my feelings as much as Derrick's. "That wound on your collarbone…"

"I'll be fine," he said. "Lockwood brought some…stuff for me in case something like this happened…"

He meant blood, of course. Faithful, prepared Lockwood. Ever the caretaker.

I did a double take as we passed a black Jaguar that was pulled over on the side of the road. My skin prickled as I made a decision. "That's the car that was following us," I said, pulling Lockwood's Maserati over to the shoulder, too. I mashed the hazards button on the dash and unlocked the doors.

"What are you doing?" Mill asked, voice escalating with each syllable.

"Just looking," I said. "I'll only be a second." I stepped out of the car. Mill groaned from the backseat. He threw open his door and struggled out of the car.

"You're sure that's the one that was following us?" he asked.

"Not many Jaguars out here in farm country," I said. "Makes it easy to recognize."

"I guess."

I looked up and down the road and hurried across the street when I didn't see headlights down either side of the long, straight, flat road.

"Where are you—" Mill asked.

The car was empty. I peered in the window, terrified that I might find a body on the backseat or something, but it was completely vacant. A half-finished coffee sat in the cupholder and the stitched briefcase that belonged to the PI was resting underneath the seat.

No blood, no signs of a struggle. Just an abandoned car. What happened to these guys?

"Cassie!" Mill shouted to me from the street.

The quiet night erupted in howls and they were uncomfortably close by.

I looked up just in time to see half a dozen werewolves burst out of the brush that lined the swampy ditch along the road, howling and snarling.

I turned and launched myself back toward the car at a sprint. I made it about two seconds before the first wolf reached me, threw myself in on the driver's side, slamming the door shut just in time. A werewolf rammed into the door, nose streaking the window with snot and fog.

I fumbled with the shifter for a second before throwing the car in drive and slammed my foot on the gas.

The werewolves that had been pushing against the sides, scratching the glass, climbing onto the roof were flung off, tumbling over and landing on the asphalt. That didn't seem to bother them, though, because I watched them rise and give chase in the rearview mirror as I floored it, hitting eighty miles an hour down that long, dark road.

In a few seconds they fell behind; apparently they couldn't keep up that pace for very long. But my stomach turned over when I saw that more than one of the werewolves had dark, wet patches that gleamed in the lamp light on their snouts and matting the fur down their front.

Blood. But from who...?

With a jolt of nausea I realized that the guys that had been following us weren't going to come out of those woods tonight...except maybe feet first.

Chapter 40

It was so late that there were hardly any cars on the highway as we made our way back toward Tampa. The whole ride was silent. Everyone was in their own heads, thinking about the night and its events.

Lockwood had come around not long after we fled, but Mill insisted that we take the two of them to his condo. He wanted to let Lockwood rest there for the night while he oversaw his recovery. "It'll be fast," Mill promised. "Fae heal quickly."

"But what about you?" I asked him.

"I'm better already," he said and he looked it. The wound had started to close over and looked almost a week old already. "I've got the things that I need to finish the job."

A well-stocked fridge at home with more blood than the local blood bank, for sure.

I dropped them off at his place without much fanfare or a goodbye. A brief kiss was all I got and a quick, "We'll talk later," as Mill helped Lockwood out toward the elevator.

I didn't know how to feel about that, but I had one last thing to do. With a heavy heart and a full head, I turned the borrowed Maserati toward Derrick's house. He was quiet the whole time and I wasn't sure that he was aware of where we were when we pulled into his driveway.

"Derrick, I..." I said, turning the car off. Even the sound of my own voice was too loud in the silent car. "I want to apologize...for everything."

He turned his face to me and I was surprised to see a curious expression there. "Apologize? Why?"

"For what happened tonight," I said. "For you getting kidnapped. For your dad turning on you like that...I just..."

"Cassie, none of that is your fault," he said quietly. "It's not like you were the one who turned him into that...that thing." His face wrinkled in pain. "And if anything, I should be apologizing to you."

"For what?" I asked.

"For being such a jerk to you," he said, running his finger over the stitching of Lockwood's seat. "I'm sorry I didn't believe you about all of this. Maybe if I had...things could have turned out differently."

I looked at the steering wheel as if it could somehow tell me the exact words to say to someone who had just lost one of their parents.

He chuckled. "You know...you just did something freaking unbelievable." He looked over at me and gave me a small, sad sort of smile. It reminded me of Iona. "You're like a miracle worker."

I snorted. "I didn't do anything," I said. "Mill, Lockwood and Jed were the ones that—"

"I'm not talking about the fight or any of that," he said. "You, Cassie, came into a super dangerous situation and risked your own life to save mine. You used a freaking rock to free me. That's ..pretty awesome."

A lump appeared in my throat and I tried to swallow it. "Well...thanks, I guess," I said awkwardly.

"No, seriously...thank you," he said. "I know that's not enough, but..."

I scratched at a piece of dried mud or something on the dashboard. It flaked as I rubbed it with my fingernail and realized it was probably better not to think too hard about what it was.

"So...are you okay? I mean...your dad..." I said. I was such an idiot. Why bring that up?

He sighed. "I'm...gonna need some time, I think. To process everything. He was wrong, obviously. He saw me as a prize to be won rather than his son. But still...he was my dad..."

I could hear the tightness in his voice, see the strain near his eyes.

"I'm sorry things ended the way they did," I said.

"Yeah…me too."

The poor guy was probably still in shock. It wouldn't really hit him until later, when he was alone, when the anger and the fear faded.

The front door to his house was thrown open and warm golden light flooded out onto the porch.

"That's Mom," Derrick said with renewed energy.

I unlocked the doors of the car and we climbed out.

"Oh, my God, my baby!" Corinna said. She was wrapped in a silken bathrobe, her hair down and tangled, the gauze bandage that Dad had put on her forehead still intact.

I smiled, but was surprised when she rushed over to me, not Derrick, throwing her arms around my neck.

"Thank you," she said through her tears. "For saving my son."

"What am I? Chopped liver?" Derrick laughed from the other side of the car.

She pulled away and smiled blearily at me through her tears before running around the car to embrace Derrick.

"If you were, the werewolves would have eaten you," I said, smiling at him over the roof of the car.

As I stood there and watched the two of them, my heart swelled with pride. I took my leave as Corinna wrapped her arms around her son's neck, wanting to give them the space they needed and I watched as they walked back inside together, their arms around one another.

Finally…something *good* had come out of my meddling. I'd managed to do what I set out to do in the first place…and that was actually helping someone.

Chapter 41

The exhaustion was starting to creep up on me as I pulled into the driveway beside Dad's car. It was the same spot where Armani suit guy had parked earlier that day.

That car would never show up here ever again, I realized with a shiver.

Mill texted me just as I was walking up to the front door, asking if I had made it back okay. I replied that I had just gotten home and that I wanted an update on him and Lockwood as soon as he could give one. He texted back saying that they were both fine. Lockwood was asleep and Mill was enjoying some O negative.

Gross.

And Cassie, if you need anything, just call, okay? I'll be up all night, after all.

I smiled at that.

I opened the door and was not surprised in the least to see both Mom and Dad sitting at the dining table, both in their pajamas. Mom jumped up from her chair when she saw me.

"Cassandra Elizabeth, I am tired of these sleepless nights because of you." But it was halfhearted, because she hurried across the kitchen to me and gave me a hug just like Derrick's mom.

I staggered under the force of it and gently patted her back with my filthy hands.

She pulled away and gave me a good one over.

"Why are you so dirty?" she asked.

"Long night," I said. "Which I spent on a farm in Sarasota."

Dad had gone past me and was looking out the front window. "A farm, huh?" He turned and gave me an accusatory look. "Where'd you get the Maserati, then?"

Mom's eyes narrowed. "You went all the way to Sarasota? So late at night?" Trust Mom to be worried about me going long distances and Dad to wonder about the car I arrived in.

"It's Lockwood's," I said. "I had to drive back, but everyone's fine. Well, everyone except Thomas's dad…"

"The werewolf?" Mom folded her arms across her chest, putting her lawyer face on. "You know we were worried sick about you."

"Yeah, well, I didn't exactly plan for everything that happened to happen," I said, walking past her to sit at the table.

"You snuck out your window," Mom said.

I sank my forehead against the table, the cool surface soothing to my aching brain. "Yeah, I guess I did. Sorry."

Mom pulled out the chair across from mine and sat down. Dad followed a moment later, finishing the half-circle of judgment now surrounding me on two sides. After a moment, she spoke...and it wasn't what I expected.

"I want to apologize for everything that happened earlier tonight," Mom said. "I'm not upset with you about what happened to our houses. We've experienced firsthand how nasty those monsters can be and even if the insurance company doesn't believe us, we know it's the truth."

I blinked at her. This was a surprise.

"What I did in response to the insurance companies coming after us was my own choice," she said, her voice quiet, almost defeated, "and it was wrong. You didn't push me to do it. I'm an adult and I will take responsibility for my choices."

Admitting her wrongs…that was hard for anyone to do. "I'm sorry, too, Mom," I said. "I keep getting involved in these things, with these people…these paranormal beings. And it's not because I'm drawn in…at least not anymore. It's because there's no one else. I just feel like I *have* to do it."

With a jolt to my heart, I realized something. Finally, something was clear to me.

"No…I *want* to do it," I said.

Mom and Dad stared at me as I started to process the words that just came out of my mouth. They were true, honest. Maybe more honest than I'd been with myself for weeks now. It was a revelation like when you first realize you're in love with someone. It was hard to admit it, but once I did…

Everything seemed to make sense.

"And, honestly, Mom? I think your legal problems might actually be solved," I said.

"What do you mean?" She wore her customary frown.

"Those guys from earlier? They followed me when I left earlier tonight," I said. "All the way out to Sarasota."

"Why?" Dad asked.

"Probably looking to see if she was up to something bad," my mother said, her brow furrowed. "That they could use as additional leverage on me."

"Well, they found something," I said. "A whole pack of werewolves. I think they got eaten, because I found their car abandoned and a whole bunch of wolves came bolting out of the woods next to it, covered in blood."

"They're dead?" She blinked a couple times, taking that in. "That's not going to solve the problem," she said, her eyes widening. "That's going to make it worse." She covered her mouth with her hands and I could almost feel the despair pulse out of her. "So much worse."

Chapter 42

The next day it was over ninety degrees with eighty-three percent humidity. Every girl in school seemed to be competing for the "Shortest shorts possible" award and all of the guys walked around with big grins on their faces and their eyes in constant motion for some reason, possibly unrelated.

But hey. At least it was Friday.

"…So, Mom doesn't think that's going to end well," I said right before sinking my teeth into another bite of my peanut butter and jelly sandwich. Childhood classic, teenage favorite.

Xandra and I were sitting out in the outdoor lunch area at a picnic table. She was happily slurping some noodles from her bright pink bento box and I was polishing off a bottle of Coke and some yogurt with my PB&J. Nearly all of the shadows had disappeared in the brightness of the noon sun.

But it was quiet. We were pretty much the only people out here braving the heat and lack of AC. Privacy was hard to come by in the cafeteria.

Xandra swirled her noodles with her chopsticks, squinting at me in the brightness. "Yeah, what if they like, frame her for murder or something?"

"No way they can trace it back to her," I said defensively, though the idea did make my stomach squirm. "Especially if there aren't any bodies to find, you know?"

We exchanged grossed out faces.

"Hey, whatcha guys talking about?" I looked up to see the smiling face of Laura, lunch bag in hand, making her way over to us.

"Werewolves," Xandra said.

Laura's face brightened. "Ooh, werewolves." She promptly sat down right beside me.

Gregory and Derrick stepped out of a side hallway a few seconds later, looking around. Gregory pointed over at us and they started making their way over. Gregory gave Derrick a very bro-like back slap and Derrick, for his part, looked...pretty normal, given what had happened.

"So, what about werewolves?" Laura asked, pulling her spinach wrap from her plastic baggie. "Because the full moon was at its peak last night, right?"

"Hey, guys," Gregory said, once they'd made it over. "Mind if me and my homie sit here?"

Xandra arched a brow at him, her noodles halfway to her mouth, frozen in midair.

"Sure," I said with a grin.

And then I realized...I suddenly had a full table.

"Hey, thanks again for everything," Gregory said, unwrapping four slices of pizza from some tinfoil. "For saving my buddy. My bro."

Derrick shot me a thankful smile from the other end of the table. "Yeah. Thanks, Cassie."

"You okay?" I asked.

He thought about it, then shrugged. "I'll make it."

That was about what I expected.

"Um, Cassie?" Laura asked. She was staring over my shoulder. "There's an Amish man lurking behind you."

Sure enough, I turned and saw Jed standing there, just beside the corner of the building, his hat in his hands. He kicked at the ground once he caught my eyes, as though willing me to come over but unwilling to ask.

"How did he get past the security officers?" Laura whispered.

"No one ever suspects the Amish of doing anything bad," Xandra said. "They could wander into a nuclear silo and the workers would be like, 'Oh, hey, yeah, just an Amish kid. No problems here. Want to see our launch protocols?'"

"Wow, so trusting," Laura said, taking a bite from her wrap.

"I'll be right back," I said, swinging my legs over the bench.

"Tell him that I want some pie from Yoder's next time he visits!" Xandra called after me.

My heart started to race the closer I got to him. I slowed my walk, trying to figure it all out before I made it over there. What was I going to say? How was I going to say it?

"Hey," he said as I drew closer.

"Hey," I said, brushing some hair behind my ear nervously.

"So…um…" he said.

"Thank you—" I said.

"I was wrong," he said at the same time.

We both paused, awkwardly. "Oh, you go ahead," I said.

"No, it's okay, you go."

"I insist," I said. My cheeks were turning pink and I wished they would stop.

"Okay," he said and then he took a deep breath. "I'm sorry. I was wrong. About…well, a lot of things," he said.

"No, I'm sorry," I said. "Seriously. That fight…it was stupid. I never should have—"

He held up a hand. "Don't worry about it, all right? I'm not upset anymore. I forgave you as soon as I walked away. I knew I let myself get all fired up and that was wrong. Wrath…well, it's against everything I believe in."

I smiled. "Well…I should thank you for saving us last night."

Jed smirked. "It was nothing."

A moment of silence passed between us.

"You know…you weren't what I thought," Jed said. "When we first met."

"What do you mean?" I asked.

"I thought you were just some love-sick girl who had no idea what she was getting herself into. But…you're strong, Cassie Howell." He kicked at the ground again. "Stronger than anyone I've ever known. To come out to our land last night, on a full moon…" He shook his head. "That's brave."

"Or stupid, maybe," I said, trying to hide what I was feeling behind a tight smile.

"I don't think so." He glanced over my shoulder at the table of people I had left. "I shouldn't keep you. I just wanted you to know that...well, I wouldn't mind seeing you again. You know, if you ever needed help or something." His face had turned red and he gave me a puppy grin.

"I'll keep that in mind," I said.

He put his hat on his head and turned to leave.

"See you soon...vampire slayer," he said.

"I'll see you later...wolf boy."

He grinned and walked off through the grass toward the parking lot.

"What do you think a fully-waxed werewolf would look like?" I heard Xandra ask as I walked back to the table.

"Incredibly bald," Derrick said. "And probably pretty pissed off, because waxing really hurts."

"How would you know that?" Laura asked and I could hear the teasing in her voice.

I joined them laughing at that, because hey, it was hilarious.

"You read these things," Derrick said, shrugging, flushing just a little. "You know. On the web."

"Suuuuuuure," Laura said.

"Hey, don't hate on a man for waxing," Xandra said, slurping down a mouth full of noodles. "Reward him for his good behavior, so we can get more of it."

"Because Xandra will not be happy until the world of the race of man is as hairless as Sphynx cats," I said and everybody laughed.

I basked in the warmth of their amusement and thought about how far I'd come in the few months since I'd come to Florida. From liar to truth-teller, from friendless to...well, sitting at a table surrounded by them.

From Cassie Howell, the girl most likely to get chased out of town by an angry mob of townsfolk for lying about...well, everything...to...what had Jed called me?

Oh, yeah. Vampire slayer.

I could get used to that. All of this, actually, I realized, as my table of friends dissolved into laughter again at some silly thing Gregory said and I joined them...content at last.

Cassie Howell will return in

HIT YOU WHERE YOU LIVE

Liars and Vampires
Book 7

Coming Spring 2019!

Author's Note

Thanks for reading! If you want to know immediately when future books become available, take sixty seconds and sign up for my NEW RELEASE EMAIL ALERTS by visiting my website. I don't sell your information and I only send out emails when I have a new book out. The reason you should sign up for this is because I don't always set release dates, and even if you're following me on Facebook (robertJcrane (Author)) or Twitter (@robertJcrane), it's easy to miss my book announcements because...well, because social media is an imprecise thing.

Come join the discussion on my website:
http://www.robertjcrane.com!

Cheers,
Robert J. Crane

ACKNOWLEDGMENTS

Thanks to Lewis Moore for editing this book. Proofing was completed by Lillie of Lillie's Literary Service (https://lilliesls.wordpress.com) and Jo Evans of Raj of India.

Cover by Karri Klawiter (artbykarri.com).

Co-authoring by Kate Hasbrouck.

Formatting by Nick Bowman (http://www.nickbowman-editing.com)

Sanity NOT by Robert J. Crane's family. But I love them anyway.

Other Works by Robert J. Crane

The Girl in the Box *and* Out of the Box
Contemporary Urban Fantasy

Alone: The Girl in the Box, Book 1
Untouched: The Girl in the Box, Book 2
Soulless: The Girl in the Box, Book 3
Family: The Girl in the Box, Book 4
Omega: The Girl in the Box, Book 5
Broken: The Girl in the Box, Book 6
Enemies: The Girl in the Box, Book 7
Legacy: The Girl in the Box, Book 8
Destiny: The Girl in the Box, Book 9
Power: The Girl in the Box, Book 10

Limitless: Out of the Box, Book 1
In the Wind: Out of the Box, Book 2
Ruthless: Out of the Box, Book 3
Grounded: Out of the Box, Book 4
Tormented: Out of the Box, Book 5
Vengeful: Out of the Box, Book 6
Sea Change: Out of the Box, Book 7
Painkiller: Out of the Box, Book 8
Masks: Out of the Box, Book 9
Prisoners: Out of the Box, Book 10
Unyielding: Out of the Box, Book 11
Hollow: Out of the Box, Book 12
Toxicity: Out of the Box, Book 13
Small Things: Out of the Box, Book 14
Hunters: Out of the Box, Book 15
Badder: Out of the Box, Book 16
Apex: Out of the Box, Book 18
Time: Out of the Box, Book 19
Driven: Out of the Box, Book 20
Remember: Out of the Box, Book 21
Hero: Out of the Box, Book 22
Flashback: Out of the Box, Book 23
Cold: Out of the Box, Book 24* *(Coming February 8, 2019!)*

World of Sanctuary
Epic Fantasy

Defender: The Sanctuary Series, Volume One
Avenger: The Sanctuary Series, Volume Two
Champion: The Sanctuary Series, Volume Three
Crusader: The Sanctuary Series, Volume Four
Sanctuary Tales, Volume One - A Short Story Collection
Thy Father's Shadow: The Sanctuary Series, Volume 4.5
Master: The Sanctuary Series, Volume Five
Fated in Darkness: The Sanctuary Series, Volume 5.5
Warlord: The Sanctuary Series, Volume Six
Heretic: The Sanctuary Series, Volume Seven
Legend: The Sanctuary Series, Volume Eight
Ghosts of Sanctuary: The Sanctuary Series, Volume Nine
Call of the Hero: The Sanctuary Series, Volume Ten* *(Coming in 2019!)*

A Haven in Ash: Ashes of Luukessia, Volume One *(with Michael Winstone)*
A Respite From Storms: Ashes of Luukessia, Volume Two *(with Michael Winstone)*
A Home in the Hills: Ashes of Luukessia, Volume Three *(with Michael Winstone)*

Southern Watch
Contemporary Urban Fantasy

Called: Southern Watch, Book 1
Depths: Southern Watch, Book 2
Corrupted: Southern Watch, Book 3
Unearthed: Southern Watch, Book 4
Legion: Southern Watch, Book 5
Starling: Southern Watch, Book 6
Forsaken: Southern Watch, Book 7
Hallowed: Southern Watch, Book 8* *(Coming in 2020!)*

The Shattered Dome

(with Nicholas J. Ambrose)
Sci-Fi

Voiceless: The Shattered Dome, Book 1

The Mira Brand Adventures

Contemporary Urban Fantasy

The World Beneath: The Mira Brand Adventures, Book 1
The Tide of Ages: The Mira Brand Adventures, Book 2
The City of Lies: The Mira Brand Adventures, Book 3
The King of the Skies: The Mira Brand Adventures, Book 4
The Best of Us: The Mira Brand Adventures, Book 5
We Aimless Few: The Mira Brand Adventures, Book 6
The Gang of Legend: The Mira Brand Adventures, Book 7
The Antecessor Conundrum: The Mira Brand Adventures, Book 8*
(Coming in 2019!)

Liars and Vampires

(with Lauren Harper)
Contemporary Urban Fantasy

No One Will Believe You: Liars and Vampires, Book 1
Someone Should Save Her: Liars and Vampires, Book 2
You Can't Go Home Again: Liars and Vampires, Book 3
In The Dark: Liars and Vampires, Book 4
Her Lying Days Are Done: Liars and Vampires, Book 5
Heir of the Dog: Liars and Vampires, Book 6
Hit You Where You Live: Liars and Vampires, Book 7* *(Coming Spring 2019!)*

* Forthcoming, Subject to Change

Printed in Great Britain
by Amazon